Megastar Mysteries

Songbird

Annabelle Starr

EGMONT

Special thanks to:

Kirsty Neale, St John's Walworth Church of England School
and Belmont Primary School

EGMONT
We bring stories to life

Published in Great Britain 2007
by Egmont UK Limited
239 Kensington High Street, London W8 6SA

Text & illustrations © 2007 Egmont UK Ltd
Text by Kirsty Neale
Illustrations by Helen Turner

The moral rights of the author and illustrator have been asserted

ISBN 978 1 4052 3247 0

1 3 5 7 9 10 8 6 4 2

A CIP catalogue record for this title is available
from the British Library

Typeset by Avon DataSet Ltd, Bidford on Avon, Warwickshire
Printed and bound in Great Britain by the CPI Group

'I like a bit of a mystery, so I thought it was very good'
Phoebe, age 10

'I liked the way there's stuff about modelling and
make-up, cos that's what girls like'
Beth M, age 11

'Great idea – very cool! Not for boys . . .'
Louise, age 9

'I really enjoyed reading the books. They keep
you on your toes and the characters are really interesting
(I love the illustrations!) . . . They balance out humour
and suspense'
Beth R, age 10

'Exciting and quite unpredictable. I like that the girls
do the detective work'
Lauren, age 10

'All the characters are very realistic. I would definitely
recommend these to a friend'
Krystyna, age 9

We want to know what *you* think about
Megastar Mysteries! Visit:

www.mega-star.co.uk

for loads of coolissimo megastar
stuff to do!

Meet the
Megastar Mysteries Team!

Hi, this is me, **Rosie Parker** (otherwise known as Nosy Parker), and these are my best mates . . .

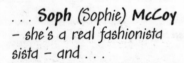

. . . **Soph** (Sophie) **McCoy** – she's a real fashionista sista – and . . .

. . . **Abs** (Abigail) **Flynn**, who's officially une grande genius.

Here's my mum, **Liz Parker**. Much to my embarrassment, her fashion and music taste is well and truly stuck in the 1980s (but despite all that I still love her dearly) . . .

. . . and my nan, **Pam Parker**, the murder-mystery freak I mentioned on the cover. Sometimes, just sometimes, her crackpot ideas do come in handy.

Consider yourself introduced!

ROSIE'S MINI MEGASTAR PHRASEBOOK

Want to speak our lingo, but don't know your soeurs from your signorinas? No problemo! Just use my comprehensive guide . . .

-a-rama	add this ending to a word to indicate a large quantity: e.g. 'The after-show party was celeb-a-rama'
amigo	Spanish for 'friend'
au contraire, mon frère	French for 'on the contrary, my brother'
au revoir	French for 'goodbye'
barf/barfy/barfissimo	sick/sick-making/very sick-making indeed
bien sûr, ma soeur	French for 'of course, my sister'
bon	French for 'good'
bonjour	French for 'hello'
celeb	short for 'celebrity'
convo	short for 'conversation'
cringe-fest	a highly embarrassing situation
Cringeville	a place we all visit from time to time when something truly embarrassing happens to us
cringeworthy	an embarrassing person, place or thing might be described as this
daggy	Australian for 'unfashionable' or unstylish'
doco	short for 'documentary'
exactamundo	not a real foreign word, but a great way to express your agreement with someone
exactement	French for 'exactly'

excusez moi	French for 'excuse me'
fashionista	'a keen follower of fashion' – can be teamed with 'sista' for added rhyming fun
glam	short for 'glamorous'
gorge/gorgey	short for 'gorgeous': e.g. 'the lead singer of that band is gorge/gorgey'
hilarioso	not a foreign word at all, just a great way to liven up 'hilarious'
hola, señora	Spanish for 'hello, missus'
hottie	no, this is *not* short for hot water bottle – it's how you might describe an attractive-looking boy to your friends
-issimo	try adding this ending to English adjectives for extra emphasis: e.g. coolissimo, crazissimo – très funissimo, non?
je ne sais pas	French for 'I don't know'
je voudrais un beau garçon, s'il vous plaît	French for 'I would like an attractive boy, please'
journos	short for 'journalists'
les Français	French for, erm, 'the French'
Loserville	this is where losers live, particularly evil school bully Amanda Hawkins
mais	French for 'but'
marvelloso	not technically a foreign word, just a more exotic version of 'marvellous'
massivo	Italian for 'massive'
mon amie/mes amis	French for 'my friend'/'my friends'
muchos	Spanish for 'many'

non	French for 'no'
nous avons deux garçons ici	French for 'we have two boys here'
no way, José!	'that's never going to happen!'
oui	French for 'yes'
quelle horreur!	French for 'what horror!'
quelle surprise!	French for 'what a surprise!'
sacré bleu	French for 'gosh' or even 'blimey'
stupido	this is the Italian for 'stupid' – stupid!
-tastic	add this ending to any word to indicate a lot of something: e.g. 'Abs is braintastic'
très	French for 'very'
swoonsome	decidedly attractive
si, si, signor/signorina	Italian for 'yes, yes, mister/miss'
terriblement	French for 'terribly'
une grande	French for 'a big' – add the word 'genius' and you have the perfect description of Abs
Vogue	it's only the world's most influential fashion magazine, darling!
voilà	French for 'there it is'
what's the story, Rory?	'what's going on?'
what's the plan, Stan?	'which course of action do you think we should take?'
what the crusty old grandads?	'what on earth?'
zut alors!	French for 'darn it!'

Hi Megastar reader!

My name's Annabelle Starr*. I'm a fashion stylist – just like Soph's Aunt Penny – which means it's my job to help celebrities look their best at all times.

Over the years, I've worked with all sorts of big names, some of whom also have seriously big egos! Take the time I flew all the way to Japan to style a shoot for a girl band. One of the members refused to wear the designer number I'd picked out for her and insisted on sporting a dress her mum had run up from some revolting old curtains instead. The only way I could get her to take it off was to persuade her it didn't match her pet Pekinese's outfit!

Anyway, when I first started out, I never dreamt I'd write a series of books based around my crazy celebrity experiences, but that's just what I've done with Megastar Mysteries. Rosie, Soph and Abs have just the sort of adventures I wish my friends and I could have got up to when we were teenagers!

I really hope you enjoy reading the books as much as I enjoyed writing them!

Love **Annabelle**

* I'll let you in to a little secret: this isn't my real name, but in this business you can never be too careful!

Chapter One

My friend Soph is fashion obsessed. She's the only person I know who gets excited about going into charity shops. She spends most of the money from her Saturday job on the kind of hideous old clothes even your nan wouldn't wear. But Soph takes them home and somehow, through the amazing power of her scissors and sewing machine, turns them into utterly gorgey designer-type outfits. Which was why, when I found myself in the middle of a serious jumper-related crisis, she was the obvious person to ask for advice, along with my other best friend, Abs, who has a brain the size of a planet.

'Auntie Muriel sent me a present,' I told them. It was lunchtime and we were in the school canteen. 'An orange jumper with a totally huge and seriously disgusting yellow bunny on the front.'

'Stylish,' said Abs.

'The thing is, Mum won't let me take it back to the shop and change it for something – oh, I don't know – an earthling might wear. She says it's ungrateful.'

'Surely she doesn't expect you to wear it?' said Abs. 'She does know you're fourteen, right?'

'You wouldn't think so from the way she treats me sometimes,' I grouched.

Abs thought for a minute. 'Maybe you could dye it or something, and stick a piece of material over the rabbit?'

We looked at Soph. That sort of thing was totally her department.

'Er, Soph?' said Abs.

But she was completely vagued out, staring

across the canteen with a fork dangling from one hand. I followed the direction of her gaze, thinking maybe James Scott, this year-twelve boy who she has a humongous crush on, had just walked in. There was no sign of him though. In fact, unless Soph had developed a very recent thing for geeky comic-reading year sevens, there was no sign of anything interesting. Abs waggled her hand in front of Soph's face.

'What?' said Soph.

'We were just saying,' said Abs, 'about Rosie's bunny jumper.'

'What?' Soph practically shouted.

Suddenly, I twigged. Like the genius mystery-solver I am, I lifted up a big chunk of her wavy brown hair and saw exactly what I'd expected to see: an earpiece, attached to the tiny pink MP3 player Soph's dad had given her for getting an 'A' in Mr Footer's science test.

Honestly, Soph is sooo spoiled. I got an 'A' in English last term and all my mum said was, 'That's nice, love. Have you seen my legwarmers

anywhere?' When I very patiently pointed out that proper parents – the kind who really love their daughters – buy presents as a reward for good grades, do you know what she said?

'I'll treat you to a chocolate-chip muffin next time we're in Trotters.'

Hours and hours of hard homeworky slog rewarded with a stingy bit of cake in an old person's café. I ask you.

I yanked the earpiece out of Soph's ear.

'Hey!' she protested.

'We're trying to have a conversation here, Soph,' I said.

'About clothes,' added Abs.

Soph frowned. You could practically see her brain whirring as she tried to work out whether sulking about the headphone thing was more important than sounding off on her specialist subject.

'What are you listening to that's so important anyway?' I asked, curious.

She pulled out the other earpiece and handed

one to Abs and one to me. I waited as Soph scrolled through the songs on her MP3 player.

'Here,' she said. 'Listen.'

'It's SongBird!' I said, recognising the tune straightaway.

'Who?' asked Abs.

'Exactly,' I said.

'Right,' said Abs. 'Great. Thanks for clearing that up for me.'

'SongBird,' I repeated. 'Haven't you seen the *MyPlace* webpage?'

Abs shook her head.

'My cousin sent me the link,' said Soph. 'The song's really cool, but I don't know anything about it except it's by SongBird.'

'*No one* knows anything about it,' I explained. 'It's this whole weird mystery. The song was posted on *MyPlace* a few weeks ago, but there's no picture on the page and no biog – just a name.'

'SongBird?' Abs suggested.

'Yep. And there's a message under the name that says, "I hope you enjoy listening to this as much as I enjoyed writing it", but that's all.'

'Weirdy beardy,' said Soph. 'Have you tried doing a search for it?'

'Do the French put garlic on their cornflakes?' I said. 'Mais oui. And not just me. Everyone wants to know who SongBird is. There's gossip all over the Internet about it.'

'What's the song called?' said Abs, listening to the earpiece again.

'"I Wish Things Were Different"' I said.

'*You can really do it, make a change. Oooh-oooh-oooh,*' sang Soph. She has a famously dreadful voice.

'If I'd written a song that good, there's no way I'd keep it quiet,' she said. 'Everyone would know it was me.'

Abs raised one of her eyebrows so high it disappeared under her fringe. 'Yep, they'd *definitely* know it was you, Soph,' she said.

Soph poked her tongue out.

'I don't think SongBird will be able to keep it quiet much longer,' I said.

Abs opened her yoghurt. 'How d'you mean?'

'Thousands of people have downloaded the song – probably hundreds of thousands by now. According to *Star Secrets* magazine, if it carries on like this, it'll soon be the most downloaded song ever.'

'That's a massivo secret to keep,' said Abs.

'Exactly,' I nodded. 'Someone's bound to find out who's behind it soon. Some nosy reporter, or maybe –'

I was about to suggest we could do some investigating ourselves, but before I could get the words out, there was a humongous crash and all three of us jumped. Soph shot a forkful of mashed potato across the table and Abs, who was still listening to the song, dropped the earpiece into her yoghurt. We whipped around to see a mousy-haired girl sitting at the end of our table, with a horrified expression on her face. She'd just knocked her tray off the table. It was upside down on the floor, along with her plate, knife, fork and a spreading pool of baked beans. Her uniform was covered in orange bean splatters that totally clashed with her red cheeks. What made me feel even worse was that it was Louise Collins. She's in the same form as me and Soph. Totally nice but, like, the quietest person I've *ever* met. Even more mousy than her hair, as Soph once said.

While we watched, Louise stood up, still looking horror-struck. Unfortunately, instead of calmly and quietly clearing up the mess, she caught her bag on the edge of the table. She stumbled backwards and this time sent her chair flying with another loud clatter. The canteen went loonissimo. Everyone turned round to stare, loads of people started laughing and there was even some clapping and cheering. Louise's face was seriously beetrooty.

'Could you be any clumsier, Colly-wobbles?' sneered a familiar voice from the next table. Amanda Hawkins: school witch and general evil-doer. Just when you thought things couldn't get any worse.

'Ignore her,' said Abs, quietly. I had this tendency to argue back with Amanda, which was never the best idea.

I didn't say anything, but went to help Louise pick up her lunch things.

'Thanks,' she said in a quiet, strangled kind of voice.

'Did you hear something?' said Amanda to her almost-as-evil cronies, Lara Neils and Keira Roberts. 'Eee-eee-eee, little mousy Colly-wobbles.' She made a squeaking noise and twitched her nose in what was supposed to be a mouse impression. How she gets all the best parts in school plays, I'll never know.

'Leave her alone, Amanda,' I said. I couldn't hold it in any longer.

'It's not my fault,' she said. 'I was minding my own business. She's the one who started crashing about, spoiling my lunch.'

'Yeah,' said Keira, sounding even dimmer than she looked.

'Y'know,' Amanda continued, 'I'm surprised. You wouldn't think a mouse like that *could* make more noise than a herd of stomping great elephants.'

Louise's face crumpled. Grabbing her bag, she ran out of the canteen.

'See you, loser!' Amanda called after her.

'That was totally hilarious,' said Lara.

'Well funny,' agreed Keira.

'Are you three sharing one brain cell today?' I said, finally snapping. 'What's funny about making someone cry?'

'I'll show you, if you like,' Amanda threatened.

'As if,' said Abs.

'Oooh, Four-eyes is getting narky now,' said Amanda. Apart from being an evil witch, she's totally thick, too. Abs wasn't even wearing her glasses.

'It must be hard,' I said in a loud voice to Abs and Soph, 'being so utterly boring, your only hobby is picking on people. You have to feel sorry for her.'

'You'll be feeling sorry if you don't shut up,' said Amanda.

I was just about to answer when I spotted Mrs Oldham (English teacher, deputy head and famous shouter) striding in through the canteen doors.

Even though I was still fuming, I knew there was no point carrying on with the argument. Mrs Oldham may have the dress sense of a line-dancer, but she has the eyes of a hawk and the nose of a police sniffer dog. She'd be over at the first sign of an argument and, knowing Amanda Hawkins like I unfortunately do, she'd sooo manage to twist things and make it all look like my fault.

No way was she having the last word, though.

'D'you want to come over here and say that?' I said.

Massivo cliché, but that stuff works on a halfwit like Amanda.

She stood up and stepped over to our table. 'Maybe I do.'

'Uh-oh,' said Abs, realising what I was up to. 'Oldham's just walked in.'

Amanda spun round and saw Mrs O looking straight at us. She quickly sat down in the seat opposite.

'I think it's time we left,' I said.

'Absolutely,' said Abs.

'OK,' said Soph, who looked a bit confused.

'Nosy, Four-eyes and the Fashion Freak,' Amanda called after us. 'You lot deserve each other.'

'That chair Amanda just sat on,' said Soph as we stacked our trays by the door, 'wasn't it . . .'

'Yep,' I grinned. 'The one your mashed potato landed on.'

✳ ✳ ✳

It's amazing how seeing a girl walk round with mashed potato on her bum all afternoon can cheer you up. Amanda Hawkins was still a complete troll, but I saw Louise by her locker just before the afternoon bell rang and she looked a bit more cheerful. She'd changed out of the bean-splattered uniform into her gym kit and her face was back to its normal colour. She gave me a small smile as she hurried past.

In fact, the only bit I found myself thinking about when I got home was the idea that we could try to find out who SongBird really was. After all, we'd solved plenty of mysteries before and this one was really interesting. Like Soph said, why would anyone want to keep quiet about writing such a cool song?

I was just thinking it over when my phone beeped. It was a text from Abs:

Turn on MTV now!

By some miracle, my Nan, who is dangerously television obsessed – murder-mystery shows in particular – was out at Trotters, so I didn't have to wrestle her for the remote control. I flipped through a couple of channels before I found the right one. And there it was, halfway through the second verse – 'I Wish Things Were Different'. I sat with my mouth open. It was definitely SongBird – I'd listened to it so many times, I'd recognise her voice anywhere – but she didn't look anything like I'd imagined. She was seriously gorgeous – tall and thin with short, wavy blonde hair and bright green eyes. She looked more like a model than a singer. The video wasn't brilliant – lots of shaky close-ups and SongBird smiling into the camera. It had obviously been done in a real rush, which made sense, considering the mystery behind it. There was something a bit odd about it all, though. When the song finished, I switched the TV off and went upstairs.

I'd visited SongBird's *MyPlace* page so often, I didn't need to look up the address. Now, instead of the almost-blank screen, there was a photo of the girl from the video, a biog and a name: Georgina Good. I scrolled down to the biog, itching to find out more about her.

Hi! It's brilliant to be able to add my pic and real name to the website at last. I'm really happy that so many people like my song. I've been writing music and singing for ages. 'I Wish Things Were Different' is about how we can all make a difference if we want to. It's good to be a bit mysterious, which is why I've been so secretive until now. See you on tour!

So that was that. I flopped back on to my bed, feeling kind of disappointed. It looked like there was no mystery for us to solve after all.

Chapter Two

The *Borehurst Chronicle* is normally the world's most boring newspaper. They have a mixture of proper stories like you see on TV and yawnsome local stuff. 'Borehurst Man in Paper-cut Drama', 'Mayor Scratches Bum in Post-office Queue' – that sort of thing. So Mrs Campbell at the newsagent's looked quite surprised when I coughed up fifty pence for one on my way to school the next morning. There was a huge picture of Georgina Good on the front page and I was dying to read the interview. I hoped it would include some juicy answers, not to mention gossip.

For once, I was early. Nan had been in one of her cleaning moods when I got up, dusting everything in sight, including the mug I was drinking from. She made me sit with my feet up in the air so she could vacuum around me. When she accidentally sprayed polish on my toast, I decided going to school was probably a better bet. Ordinarily, I'd have waited outside the gates for Soph and Abs, but it was raining and I wanted to read the Georgina Good interview, not turn it into papier mâché. I wandered into our form room, settled down in my usual seat and opened the newspaper.

Ten things I learned about Georgina Good from the *Borehurst Chronicle*:

1. She went to a stage school called Little Darlings. Her favourite subject was music, closely followed by tap dancing, because she liked the shoes.

2. She's entered twenty-three beauty competitions and won fourteen of them. Her top tip is to practise your smile in front of a mirror for at least half an hour every day.

3. Her ambition *was* to be famous. Now she *is* famous, her ambition is to marry a footballer. She would also like to achieve world peace and help sick children.

4. She loves music and writing songs. She plays the recorder, and she had piano lessons for a few months when she was seven.

5. She wrote 'I Wish Things Were Different' on holiday in Tenerife last year. She held a seashell up to her ear and the sound inspired her to write the tune.

6. She put the song on the Internet because her best friend suggested it.

7. She decided not to put up a photo or use her real name because she likes to be mysterious. SongBird was her childhood nickname.

8. She revealed her true identity because she really wanted to make a video and see herself

on TV. She's already working on ideas for her next video.

9. She's releasing an album next month. It will be called BirdSongs and she'll be wearing a silver minidress on the cover.

10. She loves Posh Spice. She also likes reality TV and if she wasn't a pop star, she'd be a model or a presenter.

I have to admit, I was kind of surprised. Stage school and beauty pageants sooo didn't sound like the SongBird I'd imagined. Georgina Good was obviously a total wannabe, and it was weird to think someone like that had written a song like 'I Wish Things Were Different'. The recording sounded as though she was singing for the love of it, not because she was desperate to get papped at the opening of a designer envelope.

'Hola, señora,' said Soph, plonking herself down in the seat next to me. I'd been so busy daydreaming, I hadn't even seen her come in. 'What's the goss?'

'Well, duh,' I said. 'Only that the whole world knows who SongBird is.'

'Oooh, I know,' she said. 'Dad gets the paper delivered. I read it at brekkie.'

'Did you see the video last night?'

She shook her head. 'Abs texted me, but we were at my uncle's. His TV's only got about three channels. It's like he's a caveman.'

'So what d'you think?' I said.

'I love her top,' said Soph, studying the photo on the front of the paper. 'And I nearly bought that exact same necklace in town the other week.'

'That wasn't what I meant, Soph.'

'I know,' she said. 'I just thought I'd get the important stuff out of the way first.'

'Don't you think it's weird?' I said. 'I mean, is she like you thought she would be?'

Soph frowned. 'Not really. I know you can't exactly tell from a song, but I sort of imagined she'd be more of a funky dress-over-jeans type with a pair of cute Mary Janes and maybe some chunky beads.'

If you didn't know Soph, that would probably sound seriously weird, but she can tell loads about people just from their clothes. It's like a gift. Me and Abs are used to it by now, although it still freaks us out when she gets spookily accurate character info from a pair of socks.

'It is a très good top,' I said. Soph's fashionitis was obviously catching. 'And she does look pretty cool.'

'How could she not be? That song is the best thing on the Internet since the site with those screengrabs of Orlando Bloom.'

I grinned. Maybe I'd been a bit quick to judge Georgina Good. So what if she'd gone to stage school and entered a few beauty competitions? It didn't make her a bad person, and Soph was right about the song.

'Did you see she's releasing an album next month?' I said.

'Yep,' Soph nodded. 'I can't wait to hear what the rest of her songs are like.'

'Me neither. I –'

And then it happened again. Huge crash behind us. JUMP! We spun round to see what the loonpants was going on. Honestly, you couldn't even have a proper gossip in this place without getting whiplash.

Louise Collins had just walked into our form room and dropped the pile of books and folders she was carrying. She blushed redder than my mum's Scorching Scarlet lipstick and scrambled about, frantically gathering them up. I wondered if the Amanda Hawkins incident had got to her – she'd never seemed particularly clumsy before – but then I remembered it was the clumsiness that had provoked Amanda. Before we could help her to pick everything up again, Mr Adams, our gorgey form teacher, walked into the room. In a flash, he'd bent down, scooped up Louise's books, carried them to her desk and checked she was OK. He is so dreamy.

'Morning, chaps,' he said to the rest of us. He dropped his briefcase down by his chair and perched on the edge of his desk, holding up a newspaper. 'Today's *Borehurst Chronicle*. Anyone read it?'

I shot my hand up in the air which, believe me, is not something I often do in class. Mr Adams's class is different, though. He's way cooler than any of our other teachers, but I also have this secret plan (well, Abs and Soph know about it) to get him and my mum together. The more he notices me, the more he might think I'm good stepdaughter material. Then, if we bumped into him in town or somewhere, I could introduce him to Mum and he'd ask her out. Of course, the other big part of my plan is to stop Mum going out in her dungarees and legwarmers, because, let's face it, someone as cool as Mr Adams is sooo not going to want a girlfriend who thinks it's 1985.

'Rosie,' Mr Adams smiled, pointing at me with his newspaper.

'It's amazing,' I began. 'That song everyone's been playing, "I Wish Things Were Different", was a huge mystery, and then last night there was a video on MTV. It turns out it's by this girl called Georgina Good and –'

'That's great,' Mr Adams interrupted, 'but I

was actually talking about the story on page five.'

Sacré bleu! Why do these things *always* happen to me? The Rosie Parker Big-mouth Express, next stop Cringeville Central.

I bent over the desk, turning to page five in my newspaper and hoping no one else could see the highly attractive beetroot blush that was spreading over my cheeks. Mr Adams opened his paper and held it up so everyone could see the headline:

LOCAL NATURE RESERVE
UNDER THREAT

He folded the paper over, cleared his throat and read the article out.

'The future of Borehurst Nature Reserve was yesterday thrown into doubt when a local developer applied for planning permission to build a large office block and shopping complex on the site. The nature reserve is home to numerous species of birds, animals and insects, as well as an abundance of plant life, almost all of which would be destroyed if these plans go ahead. Influential local building firm, Porter-McCabe, is hoping to construct office space to accommodate over a thousand staff, plus ten retail outlets. A representative from Borehurst District Council said the matter would be given proper consideration.'

Mr Adams stopped reading and looked up.

'That's awful,' said Soph.

There were lots of nods and 'yeahs' of agreement.

It sounded like a pretty terrible idea to me. OK, so I didn't spend all my spare time hanging out at the nature reserve, but I'd been there a few times. The thought of them storming in with a bulldozer and killing all the wildlife was, like Soph said, awful.

'I think so, too,' said Mr Adams.

'It hasn't happened yet, though,' I said. 'I mean, they're only planning to do it. Surely the council will say no when they find out how many animals it could kill.'

'The trouble is, Porter-McCabe is a powerful company. It's worth millions, and money has a funny way of getting people exactly what they want,' Mr Adams explained.

'You mean they'll bribe the council?' said Ella Gregory. (Her dad's a policeman, so she knows almost as much about crime and corruption as Nan.)

'Maybe,' said Mr Adams.

This was starting to sound serious.

'Isn't there anything we can do to stop them?' I said. I had a sudden image of myself, chained to the nature-reserve railings, with bulldozers all around revving their engines menacingly. 'You know, stage a protest march or something,' I added.

'Oooh, yes,' said Soph.

'That would be awesome,' agreed Ella.

Mr Adams beamed. 'I was hoping you'd say something like that.'

'Really?' I said.

'Absolutely,' said Mr Adams. He checked his watch, then leaned across the desk to take out the register. 'We haven't got time to talk about it properly now, but how about meeting up in the main hall at the end of lessons? Bring along anyone else who might want to help.'

Soph and I gathered up our books as he took the register, me still thinking about bulldozers and Soph probably working out what you wear when you're trying to save a nature reserve.

'Don't forget,' shouted Mr Adams as the bell rang and we all clattered out, 'anyone who's interested, main hall, straight after last period.'

Chapter Three

The main hall was buzzing when we arrived. Most of our form group was there. Ella Gregory was talking to a bunch of girls I knew from netball, and Louise Collins was on her own in the corner near a stack of wooden benches. I hoped she was over the clumsy thing. There were loads of people from other forms, too, including Abs. We'd filled her in on the nature-reserve story at lunchtime, after we'd finished discussing SongBird, and she was totally up for going to the meeting.

As we made our way through the crowd, I

suddenly spotted three figures standing with their backs to us. Amanda Hawkins, Lara Neils and Keira Roberts.

'What are *they* doing here?' I said. OK, so Lara looks a bit like a stoat, but aside from that, they've never shown any interest in nature.

'Maybe Amanda's finally realised she'll get more sense out of a badger than she will out of Keira Roberts,' said Abs.

Me and Soph cracked up.

'OK,' shouted Mr Adams over the noise in the hall, 'if everyone can take a seat, we'll get started.'

There was a bit of chair-scraping and clattering then, eventually, quiet. As well as Mr Adams, a couple of other teachers were sitting at the front of the hall – science boffin and owner of the world's most insane moustache, Mr Footer, our *Doctor Who*-obsessed drama teacher, Mr Lord (known to everyone – including the other teachers when they think we're not listening – as Time Lord), and Mrs Oldham, wearing one of her usual denim disasters.

'Great,' said Mr Adams. 'Well, as you know, we're here to see what we can do about saving Borehurst Nature Reserve from the money-grabbing clutches of Porter-McCabe.'

For a teacher, Mr Adams can be quite funny.

'As this is our first meeting, and we haven't had much time to prepare, I suggest we do a bit of brainstorming. The main aim is to raise awareness. Even though it was in the paper this morning, it wasn't a huge story, and not everyone reads the *Borehurst Chronicle*.'

'We need to make sure as many people as possible know the nature reserve is under threat,' chipped in Mr Footer. 'With greater public support and awareness, the council will be forced to reconsider.'

It's amazing. Even when he's talking about something I'm totally interested in, Mr Footer sounds so mind-bogglingly dull I could die of boredom.

'Keeping all that in mind,' said Mr Adams, 'I want everyone to chip in with their ideas and suggestions. Mrs Oldham will write them down for us so we don't lose track.' He pointed towards a whiteboard. Mrs Oldham stood next to it with a chunky marker pen.

'So, let's get started. Shout out anything you can think of, even if it sounds silly or impossible.'

There was total silence, like there always is when anyone asks a group of people to shout things out.

'How about a play?' said Time Lord eventually. He looked quite smug, as if we'd have to do his idea because it was the only one.

Mrs Oldham wrote 'play' on the whiteboard.

'Something with a nature theme to really drive the message home,' Time Lord added.

Mrs Oldham wrote '– nature theme' next to 'play'.

'A protest march,' I called out, sooo not keen to do a play because I'd probably end up being a hedgehog or a dandelion or something.

'Sponsored walk,' someone else shouted.

Mrs O added them to the board.

'I like the idea of a formal protest,' said Mr Footer. 'But a march is far too risky. We should write letters of protest to the council – the pupils, their parents and the teachers, too.'

Mrs Oldham wrote 'protest letters' on the board, and I fought the urge to fall into a coma.

'Anyone else?' said Mr Adams.

'A bring-your-pets-to-school day,' said Soph, who hasn't got a pet.

'A talent contest,' said Amanda Hawkins, who hasn't got any talent.

Mrs Oldham wrote them down.

'A sponsored nose-picking competition,' one of the boys shouted out.

Nearly everyone laughed.

Mrs Oldham pulled a face a bit like the one Nan did the time she found a piece of fingernail in one of her custard creams. She wrote 'school fête' on the board.

'OK,' grinned Mr Adams. 'I think we've got enough suggestions there. We just need to decide which one to go for.'

'I think a play's our best bet,' said Time Lord. 'Plenty of scope for everyone to be involved, and who doesn't enjoy a good bit of drama?'

Mrs Oldham pursed her lips and looked doubtful. 'Hmmm. I do think a school fête might be better. It only seems like five minutes since the last school play and,' – she gave Time Lord a seriously fake smile – 'you can have too much of a good thing. We could invite the local press along to a fête and drum up some extra interest.'

Mr Adams started to say something, but Mr Footer, whose wormy black moustache was wiggling about like mad, spoke over him.

'It's got to be the letters of protest. They'll really make the council take notice. Plays and fêtes are all very well, but we need to do something *serious* to make a difference.'

Time Lord and Mrs Oldham looked like they were about to argue back, but before either of them could speak, Mr Adams stood up.

'My suggestion,' he said, 'is that we do all three. We can send letters to the council, and arrange a school fête which includes a performance organised by Mr Lord. But,' he added, 'I think we could do with a bit of extra help to get people's attention. Some celebrity help, in fact.'

To my open-mouthed, goldfishy surprise, he looked at me. 'Rosie, you mentioned something in registration this morning about a singer.'

Oh, yes. Please let's remind everyone of that happy occasion.

'SongBird,' I mumbled.

'SongBird,' Mr Adams repeated. 'Yes. I think we should invite a celebrity along to the fête and, as she seems to be the star of the moment, SongBird could be just the person.'

'She'd be brilliant!' I said, the idea of meeting SongBird making me forget about that morning's cringe-fest.

'Terrific,' said Mr Adams. He paused, looking towards the back of the room. 'Yes, Louise?'

I turned round and, as if I hadn't had enough surprises for one afternoon, saw Louise Collins had her hand nervously stuck up in the air. She's normally so shy she can barely squeak a reply if someone asks her a direct question.

'It's just,' she began, shakily, 'I don't think . . . I mean, wouldn't someone like SongBird be much too busy to bother with a school fête? If we could find someone else . . . maybe there's a local celebrity who'd be more interested. We could invite them instead.'

She gripped the side of her chair and stared at the ground, as if speaking in front of so many people had totally exhausted her.

'What local celebrity?' scoffed Amanda Hawkins. It was obvious she was dying to give Louise a hard time, but didn't dare in front of the teachers.

'There was that guy who was on *The X Factor*,' suggested Ella Gregory.

'Simon Cowell?' said Soph. 'I don't think he's from round here.'

Abs giggled. 'Not him, Soph. One of the contestants. He turned up at the audition wearing a fireman's uniform and sang the most out-of-tune version of 'Material Girl' by Madonna that the judges had ever heard. Remember? He left Whitney High a few years ago.'

'He's hardly a celeb though,' I said.

'I'd ask Angel, but she's working in Australia at the moment,' said Frankie Gabriel. Her sister, Angel, is a supermodel who me, Abs and Soph once helped out of a sticky situation.

'I still think SongBird would be totally perfect,' I said.

'I agree with Rosie,' said Mr Adams.

'I bet she really cares about nature, too,' I added. 'You only have to listen to the words of "I Wish Things Were Different" to see that.'

'Let's put it to a vote,' said Mr Adams. 'All those in favour of inviting SongBird to the fête, raise your hand.'

I looked round at a sea of waving hands.

'And those in favour of a different celebrity,' said Mr Adams.

Just a couple of people, including Louise, put their hands up.

'SongBird it is,' said Mr Adams. 'So Mrs Oldham's going to organise the fête, Mr Lord will set up auditions for the play, and Mr Footer, if you wouldn't mind collecting letters for the council?'

Mr Footer nodded, wiggling his wormy moustache even more than usual.

'Which leaves me to get in touch with Georgina Good,' said Mr Adams. 'Terrific. I think that's about it. I'll get notes sent home to your parents to tell them what we're doing and let's see if we can't save the nature reserve.'

We all picked up our blazers and bags, ready to leave. I paused for a second to admire Mr Adams. He ran a hand through his already messy brown hair, which was a totally swoonsome habit he had, and started chatting to Mrs Oldham as he pulled on his jacket.

Abs and Soph had already headed for the door. As I hurried to catch up with them, I heard a voice behind me complaining.

'I can't believe we hung around with a bunch of losers who actually want to save that dump.'

'Don't blame me,' snapped a second voice, and I realised it was Amanda Hawkins. 'I thought the meeting was about the fact they're not building a proper mall. I mean, all those stupid offices and only ten shops. What's their problem?'

'It's not all bad,' said a third voice. I was pretty sure it was Lara Neils.

'How d'you work that out?'

'Time Lord's play,' said Lara. 'There's no rule that says you have to care about the nature reserve to audition for a starring role.'

'Oh, yeah,' said Amanda. You could practically *hear* the smug grin on her face.

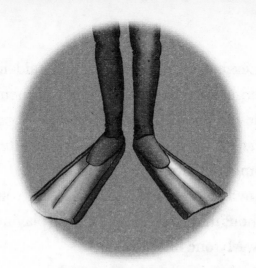

Chapter Four

Lara Neils might not be the brightest girl on the planet, but she was right about the school play. Time Lord held auditions two days after the nature-reserve meeting and, as usual, decided Amanda was 'just right for our leading role'. I nearly choked when she said she was really pleased, because saving the nature reserve was so important to her. Actually, she called it a nature *reverse*. Any other teacher would have spotted this and known straightaway she was lying her pants off. Even Time Lord would have spotted it if anyone except Saint Amanda had said it. As it was, we got a lecture about following Amanda's example and doing our best, as supporting members of the cast, to help her get the play's environmentally friendly message across.

Meanwhile, me and Abs, who both properly cared about the nature reserve, were playing a pair of frogs. My one line?:

Ribbit. [Dramatic pause.] Rrrrribbit.

Luckily for Soph, her genius sewing skills meant she had escaped the torture of rehearsals every break and lunchtime. Time Lord had made her wardrobe mistress. She spent every spare minute designing and stitching costumes. If she didn't have paint smudges on her face, she had bits of feather stuck to her leg or glitter all over her shirt, but she loved it. At the beginning of the second week, she turned up to rehearsals with a humongous grin on her face.

'What?' I said suspiciously.

'Your costumes are ready,' she said.

Oh, joy. A frog outfit. Get me Vogue *on the phone.*

'Will you try them on so I can make sure they fit?' said Soph.

* * *

'What was I supposed to say?' I asked Abs five minutes later as we stood in the girls' toilets, getting changed.

'How about "no",' said Abs from the cubicle next door.

'She spent ages making them. You saw how excited she was.'

'I s'pose,' Abs grouched. 'Zut alors, this catsuit is tight.'

'Are you ready?' I said.

'As I'll ever be.'

We both opened our cubicle doors and stepped out. I looked at Abs. She looked at me. Then we both turned and looked in the mirror.

'Soph'll be pleased,' I said faintly.

'That we look like the cucumber shelf in the

supermarket?' said Abs.

Both of us were wearing skin-tight green catsuits and flippers that Soph had painted green to match. Blobs of green paint on the catsuits were meant to look like bumpy frog's skin. Abs had a point about the cucumbers. My legs definitely had a touch of the salad ingredients about them.

'Even my mum would be embarrassed to wear this,' I said.

'How're you getting on?' said Soph, banging through the door with her sewing box. 'Wow,' she added, catching sight of us. She had a tape measure hanging from her neck like a scarf and she walked around us, examining the costumes from every angle.

'They're good,' she said, rummaging in the box. 'They just need . . . '

Something to cover up my bum, I thought. *Maybe a nice cloak I can disappear under.*

'Face paint!' she said, pulling out a jar of bright green gunge. 'We'll cover your faces and spray crazy colour in your hair. You'll need green gloves, too.'

She started scribbling in her sketchbook. Me and Abs were dumbstruck.

Just then, the door opened again.

'Er, hi,' said Louise Collins. 'Mr Adams says can you come back to the drama studio now because he's got something important to tell us. He wants everyone to be there.'

'Bien sûr!' said Abs.

'No problemo,' I added. Any excuse to get out of the cucumber suits.

We turned to go back into the cubicles.

'Um, he told me to tell you not to worry about getting changed.' Louise fidgeted nervously.

'Come on,' said Soph. 'It'll be a good chance for me to get a second opinion on the costumes.'

With me sulking and Abs fuming, we walked along the corridor to the drama studio. I say walked, but if you've ever tried to take more than two steps on dry land in a pair of flippers, you'll know it's nothing like walking. Even when people aren't accidentally stepping on the ends, it's about a gazillion times harder than trogging along in shoes.

'Gosh,' said Mr Adams, as we slunk into the room. 'Frogs. Good work, Sophie.'

She beamed. Me and Abs didn't.

'Right, if that's everyone, can I have a bit of hush?'

We were all quiet – even Time Lord, who you could tell was très annoyed about having another teacher take over his rehearsal.

Mr Adams continued, 'I've got some news and I wanted you to be the first to know, especially as you're all working so hard. I'm very happy to say Georgina Good has agreed to open the fête and perform for us.'

'No way!' yelled Soph, as everyone else started screaming and shouting too. She flung her arms around me and Abs in a weird, frog-some group hug. I was so excited, I didn't even mind that she was jumping up and down on my flippers.

'This is so cool,' I shouted over the din.

I looked round for Louise, thinking it would be nice to include her in our mini-celebration. She was standing by the door, but instead of looking happy, she had this weird look on her face, almost as though she was disgusted.

'SongBird!' shouted Abs, and forgetting about Louise, I joined in the group hug again.

'OK, OK,' smiled Mr Adams. 'Settle down. Georgina was more than happy to get involved. She's a big believer in good causes and as Rosie guessed, she's especially interested in anything to do with the environment.' He nodded at Time Lord. 'We've all got a lot of work to do before the big day, so I'll let you get back to it.'

* * *

With all the excitement over SongBird, the rest of the rehearsal was a bit useless. People kept crashing into parts of the set, and forgetting when they were supposed to come on or go off stage. Time Lord got really stroppy, which is always mucho hilarioso, because his wild, grey hair stands up and gets even wilder when he's in a bad mood.

'Concentrate!' he kept shouting. 'Rosie, will you please pay attention.'

I was. I honestly was. It was just that I forgot my cue and when I looked over at Louise, our prompt, she totally wasn't following the script or watching what was happening on stage.

Time Lord had given her the job after the auditions. She'd tried out for a part, but he didn't even make her a frog, or a non-speaking butterfly like Keira Roberts. Instead, she had to spend every rehearsal sitting at the side of the stage with the script, ready to help anyone who forgot their lines. Up until now, she'd been really good at it.

Today, though, it didn't look like she was reading the script. I could see it folded up on her lap, but there was a notebook lying open on top of it and Louise was busy scribbling in it. She was frowning as she wrote, and I got the feeling she was in her own little world. Cloud-cuckoo-land, as Nan would call it – and believe me, she should know.

'This is hopeless,' said Time Lord, rubbing his head and making the hair situation even worse. 'It was never like this when I worked on *Doctor Who*, you know. Professional actors don't get distracted by celebrities. They're just normal people – we're *all* just normal people.'

Of course we are, Cyber-loon, I thought.

'Right,' he said. 'We'll try again from the beginning of the scene. Louise, the line, please.'

I glanced across the stage. She was still writing.

'LOUISE!' barked Time Lord, and this time she did look up. Actually, she nearly fell off her chair with shock. 'If you're not too busy, can I *please* have the opening line for this scene?'

It took her a minute, flipping frantically through the script, but she finally found it and we started again.

* * *

Things got a bit better after that and we managed to get almost to the end of the play without stopping. By the time we finished, even Time Lord thought we'd done OK.

'You see what you can achieve when you put your minds to it and forget all this celebrity nonsense?' he said.

Nobody answered. We were all still thinking about SongBird.

He clapped his hands. 'Good work, people. Same time tomorrow. Louise, a word before you go.'

'Uh-oh,' whispered Soph.

'Trouble,' Abs nodded wisely.

We headed towards the door. Soph was still carrying her sewing box and Abs was flapping along in her flippers.

'Flippers!' I said, suddenly.

'Bless you,' said Abs.

'No, *flippers*.'

We all looked down at my bare feet. I'd taken the flippers off as soon as we'd finished our scene because they were a bit on the small side and really pinched my toes.

'I left them backstage,' I said. 'I'll catch up with you.'

I dashed back and ducked behind the set, trying to remember exactly where I'd left them. I hunted around a bit between some fake bushes and an old park bench, and eventually found them lying under a giant bird's nest. As I pulled them out, I heard shouting. It was coming from somewhere in front of the stage.

'It's just not good enough, Louise. We need a reliable prompt, especially during rehearsals when everyone's still learning their lines.'

There was a pause and then . . .

'I'm sorry, that won't do. I need you to be paying attention all the time. As I told you at the auditions, you might not have enough star quality to be on stage, but that doesn't mean you aren't playing an important role.'

I slowly tiptoed towards the edge of the stage, feeling kind of bad about overhearing this. Surely Time Lord didn't need to be quite so hard on Louise? I peered out and saw the two of them standing there. Louise's cheeks were red. Even from this distance I could tell she was trying not to cry.

'We'll say no more about it now,' Time Lord said. 'But remember, no one is irreplaceable. If

this happens again, I'll be forced to find another prompt.'

Louise nodded, then turned and ran out of the room. He followed her more slowly and I was on my own. I had a pretty good idea where Louise had gone. The girls' toilets were sob central. I had to go and change back into my uniform there anyway. I slipped round the side of the stage, planning to go and make sure she was OK. It was totally gloomy without the stage lights and as I passed the prompt chair, I tripped over something. It was Louise's notebook. I bent down to pick it up, thinking it must be important if she'd nearly lost her prompt job over it. But as I straightened up, the book fell open and I stared at it in shock. Written across an entire page were the words 'Georgina Good', over and over and over again, and then crossed out.

~~Georgina Good~~
~~Georgina Good~~
~~Georgina Good~~

It filled the whole page.

I am not called Nosy Parker for nothing. I know it's not exactly right to look through someone else's notebook, but I was in shock. Add that to my normal nosiness, and can you blame me for having a quick flick through it? As well as another two pages like the first one, Louise had written the words to 'I Wish Things Were Different' about twenty times – the whole song, all the way through. Her writing got messier as the book went on and the last two pages were filled with the words 'Georgina must be stopped'.

I closed the book. Something seriously strange was going on.

Chapter Five

I eventually found Louise hunched over on a bench in the yard. I'd changed back into my uniform, then come outside to track her down. The notebook was in my school bag. I didn't quite know why, but I needed to make sure no one else saw it – at least not until I'd had a chance to ask her what was going on.

'Hey,' I said, sitting down next to her on the bench.

She looked up, surprised. 'Hi.'

I fidgeted. This wasn't going to be the easiest convo of my life.

'I was in the drama studio before,' I started. 'Backstage. You know, when Time Lord was . . . I mean, I thought he was way out of order. You've been a brilliant prompt up until now.'

'Thanks,' said Louise.

'Are you OK?'

She shrugged. 'I'm fine.'

'It's just,' – I took the notebook out – 'I found this, and I honestly didn't mean to look, but it fell open and . . . All that stuff is kind of strange. I can't help thinking – worrying really – whether something's going on.'

As I spoke, Louise's face went from suspicious to panicky to furious. She stared at me for a second, then snatched the notebook.

'It's none of your business,' she snapped, gathering up the rest of her things. 'Just leave me alone.'

She stormed off, leaving me a bit stunned. Louise Collins is not the sort of girl you expect to say 'boo' to a goose, let alone 'get lost' to a part-time frog.

'Wait!' I shouted, going after her. 'Louise, I'm sorry!'

She was running now, making her way towards the school gates. I followed her round the corner, just in time to see a number 26 bus pull up to the stop.

'Louise!'

But it was too late. She pelted through the gates and leapt on just as the bus doors were closing.

Sacré blooming bleu.

'Calling Rosie Parker. Come in, Rosie Parker,' said a voice behind me, as I stood there wondering what to do next. It was Abs, closely followed by Soph.

'We've been looking everywhere for you,' said Soph. 'Why so sweaty, Betty?'

I realised I must look a bit of a state after all the rushing about and chasing. 'It's Louise,' I said. 'Something très, très peculiarissimo is going on.'

'Spill,' said Abs, her eyes practically out on stalks.

'Well, I think it's connected with SongBird,' I said.

'SongBird?' said Soph.

But right then the bell rang. It was so typical. We never got time to do anything that might actually be useful.

'Come along, girls. No dawdling,' shouted Mrs Oldham, who was on yard duty.

'Emergency meeting,' I said as we hurried back. 'Tonight, my house, nineteen hundred hours.'

'Roger, Captain Parker,' said Abs. 'Over and out.'

* * *

Abs and Soph turned up at my house bang on time. I knew they were dying to hear what had happened, and I was just as desperate to tell the story. However many times I turned it over in my brain, it didn't make any sense.

'I'll get it!' I yelled, rolling off my bed as the doorbell rang.

But Mum beat me to it. She was expecting her date – this bloke called Brian who she's been going on about all week. I was a bit annoyed, actually. I mean, she didn't know about my Mr Adams plan, but why she had to go out with some random man she met in the supermarket, I had no idea. It wasn't that I didn't want her to be happy, I just thought she should give the whole meeting-and-falling-in-love-with-Mr-Adams thing a go first.

'It's just dinner – no big deal,' she'd said, when I suggested she should be a bit more picky. So that'd be why she'd used up practically an entire tube of Scorching Scarlet lippy and decided to wear her favourite electric-blue top.

She wafted along the hallway, reeking of Bella d'Amore perfume, and checked herself in the mirror before opening the door.

'Liz Parker, I am here to arrest you on suspicion of looking gorgeous,' said the tall, bald man standing on the step.

I kid you not.

'Brian,' Mum giggled. 'I'll grab my coat.'

She wafted back along the hall and scooped up her handbag and jacket.

'See you later, Rosie, love,' she said. 'Bye, Mum,' she called to Nan, who was in the lounge watching *Diagnosis Murder*.

'Have a smashing time,' said Nan. She had obviously never seen Brian.

I was just about to close the front door when Abs and Soph walked up the path.

'Hiya girls,' Mum trilled.

'Hey, Mrs P,' said Soph.

'Who's he?' Abs mouthed at me.

I stepped to one side and let them in.

'So?' said Abs.

'Brian,' I said. 'Mum met him in the supermarket last week. I think she said he was a policeman. Either that, or he's the world's most unfunny comedian.'

'He's not a patch on Mr Adams,' said Soph. 'His jeans had creases down the middle and he's got a serious nose-hair problem.'

'Gross!' said me and Abs together.

The two of them followed me into the kitchen.

'Double chocolate-chip?' I suggested, pulling a

tub of ice cream out of the freezer.

'Si, si, signor,' said Abs, enthusiastically.

Soph found three spoons and we settled down at the table.

'So, what's the story, Rory?' said Soph, licking her spoon.

I filled them in on everything that had happened with Louise at rehearsal – her face when we heard SongBird was opening the fête, the argument with Time Lord, the stuff in her notebook and how she'd reacted when I confronted her about it.

'Oooh, la, la,' said Abs, when I'd finished.

'Blimey,' added Soph.

'That is a bit of a head-scratcher,' said Nan.

Me, Abs and Soph jumped.

'You shouldn't creep up on people like that, Nan,' I said. 'And you shouldn't listen in on their conversations, either.'

'Stealth tactics,' said Nan, tapping her finger against the side of her nose.

She really is loco.

'The thing I don't get,' said Abs, dragging us back to the Louise situation, 'is why she wrote those lyrics in her notebook so many times. If you really don't like someone, why would you do something that keeps reminding you of them?'

'It's a seriously freaky thing to do, even if you're a fan,' I said.

'There are plenty of people I don't like,' said Soph, 'but I just ignore them. My rough book hasn't got pages and pages of "Amanda Hawkins" written down and crossed out.'

Nan was crashing about, making a cup of tea.

'It's like a film I saw the other night,' she said. 'It was one of those smashing Inspector Peterson mysteries. *Love You to Death*, I think it was called. Custard cream, anyone?'

She offered round a packet of biscuits.

'Nan,' I said, warningly.

'Anyway,' she carried on, 'in the film there was this chap who was in love with his favourite singer. He got a bit carried away – he was obsessed, according to Inspector Peterson – and in the end he kidnapped her. Took her back to his house and kept her there, a prisoner.'

She squeezed out her teabag and dropped it in the bin.

'Dreadful ordeal.' She shook her head.

'Nan,' I said, as we sat there, a bit stunned. 'Are you saying Louise might be a deranged fan?'

'Heavens, no,' said Nan. 'That school of yours is ever so nice. I doubt they'd let someone deranged in. Besides, surely the poor girl's parents would have noticed. No, it sounds to me like she's just confused. A big fan of this Bird Song thingummy-jig, and doesn't know what to do about it.'

'What did you say she'd written on the last few pages of the notebook?' asked Abs.

'"Georgina must be stopped",' I said.

'You don't think . . . ' said Abs.

'She wouldn't,' said Soph.

'But why else would she write that? We can't just sit around and wait to see if she does something,' I said. 'What if Nan's wrong and she *is* deranged?'

'I have been wrong before,' Nan admitted in a not-at-all helpful or comforting way.

'If she *is* planning anything, Saturday's the perfect opportunity,' I said.

'What's Saturday?' said Nan.

'The school fête,' I said.

'The one SongBird is opening,' said Soph.

Nan trotted over to the fridge and slid a piece of paper out from under a banana-shaped magnet. 'The fête in this letter?'

'Yes,' I said, recognising Mr Adams's note.

'It doesn't mention anything about a singer,' said Nan, reading it.

'Mr Adams only found out she could come today,' I said.

'A-ha!' said Nan, triumphantly. 'When was it you saw this Louise girl writing in her notebook?'

'At rehearsals,' I said, suddenly realising what Nan was getting at, '*after* Mr Adams told us Georgina Good would be opening the fête.'

'She only started writing that stuff once she knew she'd get the chance to meet Georgina,' said Abs.

'The chance to "stop her", whatever that means,' I said.

'This is getting seriously creepy,' said Soph.

'We've got to talk to Louise,' said Abs. 'We'll find her tomorrow and sort it out. There's probably a really simple explanation.'

But it didn't sound like she believed herself.

Chapter Six

I arrived early at school again the next morning. I'd be getting a reputation as a total keeno, which, considering the way Amanda Hawkins treats such people, would not be a good thing. As well as wanting to escape from Mum, who was in an annoyingly cheerful mood after her date with Unfunny Brian, I thought me and Soph might get a chance to talk to Louise in registration. Soph obviously had the same idea, because I bumped into her outside our form room. We were the first two people there. For once, we hardly said a thing, just stared at the door and twitched every time anyone came in. Considering there are 34 people in our form group, the twitching was totally out of control by the time Mr Adams arrived. There was no sign of Louise, though, and Mr Adams marked her absent on the register.

'Maybe she had a dentist's appointment or something,' said Soph as the bell rang.

But there was still no sign of her at morning break, even though me, Abs and Soph trawled the whole school looking for her. We mentioned the dentist theory to Abs, who agreed it was possible, but also pointed out that Louise only had the one set of perfectly normal-sized teeth, and even a seriously slow dentist wouldn't take this long to sort them out.

'She's definitely off school, and there's definitely something fishy about it,' said Abs.

Soph frowned. 'D'you reckon she'll be back tomorrow?'

'Hang on a minute, Soph, I'll just consult my crystal ball,' I said.

'There you go,' said Abs. 'That's what's going to solve this problem – sarcasm.'

'Au contraire, mon frère,' I said. 'What's going to solve this problem is talking to Louise, and if we can't do it here we'll just have to go to her house.'

'Good thinking, Batgirl,' said Soph. 'We could go at lunchtime.'

'Brilliant idea,' said Abs. 'Do either of you know where she lives?'

Me and Soph looked at each other. 'No.'

'It's a good job I do, then, isn't it?' said Abs.

'How?' said Soph.

'Her house is a few streets away from mine. I've seen her on the way home from school.'

'Abs, you're a total legend,' I said.

✳ ✳ ✳

The three of us met up by the school gates at lunchtime. Much to Soph's horror, it was raining.

'My hair!' she wailed, and kept wailing most of the way to Louise's house. 'I'm going to be a total frizz-head. If James Scott sees me this afternoon, he'll think I'm such a loser.'

'It's cute,' I lied.

After about ten minutes, Abs suddenly stopped.

'This is it,' she said, quietly. 'That house there with the blue door.'

I looked across the street. 'The one with the suity bloke walking up the path?'

'Yep,' said Abs. 'That really suspicious-looking suity bloke who's wearing sunglasses in the rain and ringing Louise Collins' doorbell.'

I grabbed her and Soph and pulled them both down so we were crouching behind a big black car. Just in time too because, as we peered around the front of the car, Louise opened the door. The man in the sunnies looked up and down the street, then stepped inside the house.

'What was that about?' said Abs.

'I don't know,' I said, 'but could he have looked any shiftier?'

'I wonder if he's the reason Louise stayed off school today?' Soph said.

'I've got a feeling that if we find out what he's

doing here, it could make sense of everything,' I said.

'But how are we meant to find out?' said Abs.

I thought for a minute. We were getting seriously soaked. Outside Louise's house, there was a low hedge with a massive tree at one end. Not only might we hear what the man said when he came back out, we'd also be able to shelter under the tree.

'We need to make a run for it,' I told Abs and Soph. 'That hedge is big enough for all three of us to hide behind.'

'He could be in there for hours,' argued Abs. 'We've got to get back to school by the end of lunch.'

'It does look a bit drier over there,' said Soph, trying to flatten her frizzed-up hair with her hands.

'Fine,' said Abs. 'But we're only staying until quarter past.'

I checked that the coast was clear. We were obviously the only people who thought it was a good idea to be out in this weather, because there was no one else around. I motioned the others to follow me, and we scuttled across the road to Louise's house.

'Now what?' said Soph, as we all crouched back down.

'Ssshh!' I said, listening.

Abs must have heard something too, because she froze. If anyone found us, we were toast.

On the other side of the hedge, we heard faint voices, then the sound of a door opening. Louise was obviously letting the man out again.

'Remember,' we heard him say, 'if you see me on Saturday, you don't know me.'

'Right,' said Louise, dully.

'It's vital no one connects us if we're going to get away with the Georgina situation.'

'Fine,' Louise repeated. 'I don't know you, you don't know me.'

'Exactly,' said the man. 'Right, I'll see you on Saturday. Or not, as the case may be.'

He chuckled at his own joke. From the

slamming noise the door made, I guessed Louise wasn't splitting her sides laughing. The man walked down the path and me, Abs and Soph held our breath. I don't think I've ever kept so still.

By a massive stroke of luck, the man turned in the opposite direction when he reached the pavement. He had a large brown envelope under his arm, which I was sure he hadn't been carrying on the way in. Whistling, he walked along the street to a sleek silver sports car, zapped it open, threw the envelope on the dashboard and roared away in a cloud of environmentally unfriendly fumes.

'Talk about lucky,' said Soph. 'I so thought we were going to get caught.'

'Me too,' admitted Abs.

'Did you see the envelope?' I said.

They nodded.

'What was in it, d'you reckon?' said Abs.

I frowned. 'You don't think . . . I mean, I know it's far-fetched, but after what Nan said the other night . . . Louise wasn't paying him to kidnap Georgina Good, was she?'

'Zut alors,' said Soph.

Abs was quiet for a minute.

'It *does* sound far-fetched,' she agreed, 'but it totally explains why they can't be seen together, or act like they know each other on Saturday.'

'And the way they called it the "Georgina situation",' I said.

Incredibly, it seemed the most obvious explanation for everything.

'So, are we going to talk to Louise, or what?' said Soph.

'A crazy stalker who's probably plotting to kidnap a pop star and who I've already cheesed off this week?' I said. 'Of course we are.'

* * *

'You knock,' said Soph, when we got to the door.

'You're not *scared*, are you, Soph?' Abs teased.

'As if.'

Abs banged on the door and Soph elbowed her in the ribs.

There was no answer.

'Try again,' I said. 'We know she's in.'

Soph knocked this time, but there was still no answer.

Something in one of the downstairs windows caught my eye. The curtains were moving. I stepped backwards to get a better look and saw Louise peering out. As soon as she realised I'd seen her, she disappeared again.

I crouched down and opened the letterbox.

'Louise, I know you're in there,' I shouted through it.

'You're good,' said Soph.

'Determined,' Abs agreed.

'Louise!' I called again. 'We can help you, but only if you open the door.'

A second later, I landed on my knees in front of her. She'd pulled the door open, which was good, but while I was still holding the letterbox, which was less good. I stood up, brushing the dust off my school tights.

'Louise,' I said. 'Hi.'

'How are you feeling?' Soph asked.

Louise looked awful. She'd been crying, and instead of being blush-red like she usually is at school, her face was really pale.

'How did you find out where I live?' she said.

'Abs walks home the same way,' Soph told her. 'We were just worried because you weren't in school.'

'Please,' said Louise. 'Go away.'

'We want to help you,' I said.

'Well, you can't,' she said flatly. 'No one can.'

'How do you know unless you tell us what's wrong?' said Abs.

Louise rubbed her forehead, as if she had a bad headache. 'You wouldn't understand.'

'But we know about SongBird,' I told her. 'We know something's going on.'

'Leave me alone,' she said, suddenly sounding angry again. 'I told you yesterday, just LEAVE ME ALONE.'

And without waiting for a reply, she slammed the door, right in our faces.

Chapter Seven

On Saturday morning we had another emergency meeting at my house. Louise hadn't been back to school all week. When I'd asked Mr Adams about it, he just said she was off sick.

'Kidnapper-itis,' Abs suggested, darkly.

The trouble was, we had no actual proof Louise was up to anything.

'Maybe she won't turn up this afternoon,' said Soph.

We were all sitting round the kitchen table, and Nan was washing up the breakfast things. Mum was at the supermarket, buying stuff to make dinner for Unfunny Brian. I was quite glad, actually. A few mouthfuls of Mum's cooking, and most people run a mile. However, it did mean there was no chance of me playing matchmaker for her and Mr Adams at the school fête. It's not unknown for her to take a full day to get ready for a date and, what with dinner on the cards too, well, let's just say I was glad to be getting out of the house. There's only so much a daughter can take.

'I overheard Time Lord telling Mr Adams that Louise is still going to be prompt for the play,' said Abs. 'He hasn't found anyone else to do it.'

'At least if Louise is on stage, she won't be able to get to Georgina,' I said. 'I know she'll be out of sight of the audience, but *we'll* be able to see her. With all those people around, there won't be much she can do.'

'Actually,' said Abs, 'as long as we know where Louise is, and don't let her out of our sight, Georgina should be safe.'

'Ah,' said Nan, 'but that's where Louise's

henchman comes in. While you and the audience are distracted, he slips off and –'

She mimed cutting someone's throat, drawing a finger across her neck.

'Thanks, Nan,' I said. 'This is real life, you know, not one of your murder-mystery shows.'

'I'm just saying, it's not only Louise you've got to watch.'

I put my head down on the table, feeling totally desperate. 'How are we meant to watch both of them? Me and Abs are in the play, and Soph's the wardrobe mistress. We can't just run off if we spot him in the audience.'

'No, but I could,' said Nan, peeling off her rubber gloves.

'Really?' I said.

Inviting Nan to public events, especially at school, isn't something I'd normally do, but this might be a matter of life and death. For once, her murder-mystery obsession and extreme nosiness could be humongously useful.

'You'll help us watch them?' I said.

'Of course,' said Nan, beaming. 'Nice bit of surveillance. I've just got time to run a duster round the lounge, and then we can be off.' She trotted out of the room, still talking. 'Might be an idea to get there early and case the joint . . .'

What's that I can feel hanging in the air? Oh, yes. Impending doom.

Eight entirely rubbish things about school fêtes:

1. Raffle tickets – stupid bits of paper that let you win prizes that are mostly useless. If there are any good prizes, they are always won by people like Amanda Hawkins.
2. Megaphones – there's this modern invention called a microphone that makes your voice sound the same as normal, but louder. At fêtes, they use megaphones, which make you sound like a shouty Dalek.
3. Granny cakes – old people, mostly nans, bake cakes for the cake stall. These are lopsided,

hopeless-looking affairs you probably wouldn't take if they were free. At fêtes, people pay *pounds* for them and pretend they look delicious.

4. Teachers in their weekend clothes – too embarrassing for words. Do they all live in houses without mirrors? I nearly died laughing at the sight of Mr Footer wearing jeans and a death metal T-shirt.

5. Bunting – utterly pointless triangle-shaped flags on a string that people always put up at fêtes although no one knows why.

6. Candyfloss – tooth-rotting pink stuff that tastes of clouds and NEVER comes off your best top when stupid boys barge into you. Also, like lettuce, it is so piffling you can eat about three tons of it and still feel hungry.

7. The lucky dip – what is lucky about sticking your hand in a giant bucket of hamster sawdust and pulling out someone's manky old piece of pre-chewed chewing gum?

8. Balloon animals – bendy bits of rubber that

never look like the animal they are supposed to. Made by adults who are far too jolly for their own good and also think mime is a brilliant thing. (It is not.)

'Isn't this smashing?' said Nan, gazing around as we arrived. 'Look – a coconut shy. When I was a girl, a fair came to town every year, and I was a dab hand at the coconut shy.'

She squinted one eye and pretended to throw something at the coconuts.

I love Nan, really I do, but sometimes she totally does my head in. Abs and Soph tried hard not to giggle.

'Nan, focus,' I said, sounding horribly like Time Lord. 'Remember why you're here.'

'Of course, dear.'

'Think Jessica Fletcher or Miss Marple,' I said. It was a tried and tested trick with Nan. Get her to imagine she's one of her murder-mystery heroines and she's even more hawk-eyed than Mrs Oldham.

'We'd better go,' said Abs, checking her watch. 'The play starts in twenty minutes. Time Lord's probably got a search party looking for us already.'

'You pootle off and break a leg,' said Nan. 'I'll be fine, all ready for action out here.'

'You're sure you know who to look out for?' I checked.

'Louise is about the same height as you, with long mousey brown hair, probably wearing jeans and a T-shirt.'

'And the shifty man?'

'Tall, fair hair, stick suit —'

'SLICK!' all three of us shouted.

'Slick suit,' said Nan, 'sunglasses and a silver sports car. Got it.'

Not at all sure she had got it, we hurried off to get changed.

* * *

Soph was in her element, fixing everyone's costumes. Me and Abs had got used to looking like cucumbers. Soph came round to check our green make-up. Then we took our places on the stage.

'No sign of Louise yet,' I whispered to Abs.

She followed my gaze to the side of the stage. 'I hope Time Lord finds a replacement,' she said. 'Lara Neils keeps messing up her only line, and it's my cue to ribbit.'

'I wonder if Louise decided not to go ahead with the kidnapping after we turned up at her house,' I said. Maybe we'd been worrying about nothing.

'I don't know if you *can* change your mind once you've paid a hired goon to do it,' said Abs.

'Hired goon?'

'Thug,' said Abs. 'Criminal. That's what Mr Shifty looked like, anyway. You said it yourself.'

I could hear the audience taking their seats in the hall through the stage curtains. I caught sight of Soph in the wings, making a last-minute adjustment to Amanda Hawkins's costume. She flashed me an evil grin. A second later, I heard Amanda squeal, 'OW!' They were too far away for me to catch what Soph was saying, but she had this fake apologetic look on her face and I definitely caught the words 'pin', 'slipped' and 'accident'. Luckily for Soph, Time Lord appeared before Amanda had a chance to get properly nasty. Soph scurried away, taking her pins and tape measure with her, and Time Lord said something to Amanda, who suddenly got all false-smiley.

'Five minutes, people,' he hissed at the rest of us.

'You know, I'd almost be bothered to learn to sew if it meant I could stick pins in Amanda Hawkins,' said Abs.

I grinned and looked back across the stage, expecting to see Amanda, but she'd disappeared. Instead, with a sudden lurching in my stomach, I saw a small figure slipping into the prompt chair.

'There's Louise!' I whispered to Abs.

Abs turned round on her lily pad. 'She still looks a bit pasty.'

'At least we can keep an eye on her now,' I said. I was feeling a strange mixture of relief and nervousness, neither of which had anything to do with the play being about to start.

'Stand by,' whispered Time Lord.

He signalled to Mr Footer, who was operating the curtains. They slowly slid back, and we were off.

Once things got going, I had plenty of time to watch Louise. My big scene – the one with the ribbit line – was about halfway through. All I had to do at the start was sit on the lily pad and open my mouth in a silent, croaking sort of way every now and then. As things turned out, it was more like a silent, croaking, totally nervous sort of way, because before the first scene had even finished, I could tell Louise was up to something. Every time I looked at her she was fidgeting like mad, checking her watch or manically drumming her fingers on the script. When the lights came up on her side of the stage, you could see she was really sweating, too. As a person managing perfectly well not to sweat in a skin-tight catsuit, face paint and plastic flippers, I knew it wasn't anything to do with the temperature in the hall. It just made me even more certain trouble was brewing.

A couple of times, Abs and I swapped worried glances. I was starting to feel as uncomfortable as Louise looked. If we could just get the play over and talk to her, I knew we could sort things out. OK, so she didn't actually *want* to talk to us, and kept saying we couldn't help, but I'm not that easily put off. I thought of what Abs had said about the hired goon, and wondered if he was the reason Louise was so twitchy. Maybe all she'd said was that she didn't like SongBird, and he'd got carried away. If he was as shifty as he looked, you wouldn't want to argue with him.

'Ribbit, ribbit, ribbit,' said Abs.

I almost croaked myself. Had we got this far already? I waited a moment for my cue.

'If you keep dumping oil in the pond, what'll happen to the wildlife?' Amanda said.

'Ribbit.' My pause was VERY dramatic. 'Rrribbit.'

And that was it. Me and Abs were now set decoration. If frogs had thumbs, we'd have been twiddling them. We carried on with the odd silent croak, but we were really just waiting for the end of the play now.

'How can you be so heartless?' I heard Amanda Hawkins say in a serious bit of over-acting.

Then there was a sort of ringing silence. Ha! Amanda Hawkins, future Oscar-winner according to Time Lord, had forgotten her lines. She looked across the stage towards Louise and her script.

'I, um, I can't believe it of you, Councillor Jones,' said Amanda in a very stiff, awkward way. Even I knew that wasn't her next line. What was Louise playing at?

I glanced over and felt a sudden surge of panic. The prompt chair was empty. Louise had disappeared.

Chapter Eight

My head was spinning. The play went on for another ten minutes, and who knew what Louise could do in that time? I'd seen enough films to know a good kidnapping only takes a jiffy once you've done all the planning. Blanket over the head, bit of rope round the arms and legs, into the boot of the getaway car and Bob, as Nan would say, is your uncle.

Nan!

I peered out into the audience, totally forgetting to do any silent croaking, and scanned the rows of faces. For a second, I wondered why I hadn't looked earlier. The hired goon could be sitting out there and we were meant to be keeping an eye on him, too. Then again, he was probably waiting outside for Louise with his shiny silver getaway car, empty boot at the ready.

Finally, I spotted Nan. She was about five rows from the front and had cleverly bagged an end-of-row seat – either that, or she'd crept in late after sneaking off to the coconut shy. I wiggled about on my lily pad, frantically trying to get her attention.

'Nan,' I mouthed.

She had a vague look on her face.

I tried a small, frog-ish jump. From the wings, Time Lord glared at me threateningly. I didn't care. I looked back at Nan. Suddenly, she was staring right at me.

Hoping she'd guess what I meant, I jerked my head towards the side of the stage and opened my eyes really wide with a panicky expression. It didn't take much acting. Nan gave me a thumbs-up and slipped out of her seat.

'What's the plan, Stan?' Abs asked the second we came off stage.

'Georgina's due to arrive any minute,' I said. 'We might be too late, but we've got to try and find Louise.'

'I'm all over it,' said Soph, appearing behind us. 'There's no time for you to get changed, and those flippers weren't made for mystery-solving.' She held up two pairs of trainers. 'I thought you could use these.'

'Soph, you're a genius,' I said, kicking off my flippers.

Me and Abs tugged our trainers on and the three of us ran out of the hall.

'Over there,' I said, pointing at the temporary stage Mr Adams had set up on the sports field. He'd told us at registration on Friday that he'd arranged it through an old friend in the music industry. Me and Soph thought this sounded totally glamorous, until he explained his friend was a roadie, which basically means carrying stuff and growing a beard. But he did know loads of people who had proper stage equipment, and he'd built this amazing stage with lights, speakers, and even a backstage where Georgina could change and do some showbiz relaxing. There was already a massivo crowd of people gathered around it. I suspected wherever Georgina was going to be, we'd find Louise and the hired goon.

'Maybe we should split up,' I said, as we dashed across the field.

'Good thinking, Batgirl,' said Abs. 'Me and Soph'll go backstage – you look in the crowd.'

She swerved off around the edge of the field and Soph followed, leaving me on my own. The crowd was buzzing. Everyone seemed totally excited about Georgina. I looked around, hoping to catch sight of Louise, but with so many people, mostly facing away from me, it seemed impossible. I stood on tiptoe, craning my neck to get a better view. This girl from Abs's form gave me a really weird look. For a minute, I wondered what she was staring at. Then I remembered I was still wearing the frog costume and green face paint.

'I'm a frog,' I said, staring back at her. 'You don't think we like pop music?'

She stepped backwards, as if I had a contagious disease. I did have quite a few painted-on warts, but I got the feeling it was the bonkers-ness she was worried about catching. I grinned at her, and shuffled forward to stand in the spot she'd just left. Suddenly, I could see more faces; people who'd had their backs to me before. In a flash, I realised if I was going to find Louise, or the hired goon, it wasn't going to be by walking round the outside of the crowd. I had to get right into the middle.

'Excuse me,' I said, loudly.

A couple of the people standing just in front of me turned round. As soon as they saw my green face and body, they stepped back, just like the first girl. I moved forward, and scanned the faces I could see. Quite a lot of them actually turned around to stare at me, which made it even easier.

'Excuse me,' I said again. 'Frog coming through.'

In a surprisingly short space of time, I found myself bang in the middle of the crowd. I was about to say excuse me for the ninth or tenth time, when a boy standing in front of me said, 'Hey! It's Meanie Greenie.'

And it was. Mrs Green, our headmistress, had just walked on to the stage.

'Ladies, gentlemen and students,' she said. 'It is with great pleasure that I welcome you all to the Whitney High School Fête, in aid of Borehurst Nature Reserve. A few weeks ago, as I'm sure many of you know, a story appeared in our local newspaper regarding the future of the nature reserve.'

As she spoke, I carried on scanning the crowd. Louise probably wouldn't stop whatever she was planning while Meanie Greenie was making one of her famously long speeches.

'Excuse me,' I said, and stepped forward again. I did a quick scan, and found nothing. I tried again, looked all around and then . . . YES! Finally, I saw a familiar brown head. Louise was looking up at the stage. From where I was standing, I could just see the side of her face. She was at the very front of the crowd. As I watched, I realised she was in a sort of daze. Unlike everyone else in the over-excitable crowd, she was totally still. No way was I going to let her get away again. I needed to get to the front, and quickly, which meant no more Ms Nice Frog. I started to push towards the front of the stage, heading for Louise.

'. . . to make even more people aware of the nature reserve's plight, we decided to invite a celebrity guest along. Our students nominated Georgina Good – SongBird,' Mrs Green was saying.

At the mention of SongBird, the crowd went crazy and surged forwards.

'Hey!' I shouted, totally pointlessly.

In the crush, I lost sight of Louise, but I still knew more or less where she had been, so I carried on pushing forward. It was much harder now. Everyone else had done the same thing, and I said sorry about a thousand times for stepping on people's feet or bumping into their elbows. Meanie Greenie lulled the crowd back into a snoozier mood with the rest of her speech and eventually I reached the front. I looked around, ready to grab Louise, but there was no sign of her. I checked my position. This was definitely where she'd been. Even if the surging crowd had moved her about, I should still have been able to see her. The truth was, I'd lost her again.

I gazed up at Meanie Greenie, wondering what to do next – also wondering how long she could keep going before the crowd started booing or, if she was very unlucky, throwing fruit. Just then, something at the side of the stage caught my eye. It was only the quickest glimpse, but it was enough. Louise was heading backstage.

* * *

'Afraid I can't let you through, miss,' said Ella Gregory's dad, who'd voluteered to act as one of the fête security guards. I'd run after Louise. There was no sign of her now, and nowhere else she could have gone, so she had to be inside. What had she said to Mr Gregory to get past him? I thought quickly.

Wanted: one genius excuse guaranteed to persuade security that I, Rosie Parker, super-sleuth, future megastar and temporary frog, should be allowed backstage.

Top three possibilities:

1. I'm a journalist, here to interview Georgina Good.
2. I'm the tea lady, here to make Georgina Good a nice fresh pot of tea with some biscuits.
3. I'm from the local beauty salon, here to give Georgina Good a makeover.

Chances of success:

1. Nil. I have no notebook, no pen and why would a journalist be dressed like a frog?
2. Nil. No tea, no pot, no biscuits and why would a tea lady be dressed like a frog?
3. Nil. No make-up, no hairbrushes and why would a beautician be dressed like a frog?

'I'm a frog,' I said to Mr Gregory. 'Well, not a real one, obviously.'

He stared at me.

'I'm from the welcoming committee,' I carried on. 'You know, cos Georgina's so cool, helping out on the nature-reserve front. We decided to dress up to welcome her to Whitney High and say thanks for coming.'

'I don't know . . .' He sounded hesitant.

'Really,' I said persuasively, 'would I be walking round looking like a frog for fun?'

'I suppose,' he said. There was a pause. 'Oh, all right. On you go.'

He stepped aside and, relieved, I scooted past.

Backstage was way less glamorous than I'd imagined. It was dark and gloomy. Although there were doors that looked as though they led to dressing rooms, most people were milling about in the cramped space just off the stage.

As I stood there, I heard Mrs Green winding up her speech, which meant she was about to introduce Georgina. Time was running out and I couldn't see Louise anywhere. I was just about to check the dressing rooms, when two things happened. Firstly, Georgina Good drifted past me on her way to the stage. Secondly, I saw the hired goon. He was still wearing his sharp suit, but this time without the sunglasses.

When Meanie Greenie announced Georgina's name, everyone else backstage leapt into action – some heading for the stage, others hurrying to shift pieces of equipment.

The goon didn't move. His eyes narrowed as he watched Georgina. Without looking away, he reached into his pocket and, to my horror, pulled out something small, black and metallic.

ZUT ALORS!

'Stop him!' I shouted. 'He's got a gun!'

And without really thinking, I hurled myself forward.

Chapter Nine

It was quite surprising. The goon was enormous, but I must be stronger than I thought, because we both crashed to the ground. Everything went a bit barmy. People were rushing around and shouting. The next thing I knew, I was being picked up by Mr Gregory. And when I say picked up, I mean it. He grabbed me round the middle and tucked me under his arm then, with his free hand, he signalled for the other security guards to grab the goon before he could escape.

'It's OK, he's secure,' said the chief guard,

snapping a pair of handcuffs on the goon, who was face down with his hands behind his back and his nose squashed against a pile of dusty cables.

'Floored by a frog, eh?' said Mr Gregory to the man, finally putting me down.

'Er, chief,' said the youngest-looking guard.

The one who'd handcuffed the goon was clicking his walkie-talkie.

'What is it, Flannigan?' he said.

'The gun, chief.'

'What about the gun?'

Flannigan picked it up. It had skidded away when I knocked the goon over. Except, now Flannigan was holding it out, it was totally obviously not a gun at all.

'It's a mobile phone, chief,' said Flannigan.

OH.

QUELLE.

HORREUR.

I mean, it was a small, thin, black, metallic phone – not *that* different to a gun, especially in the almost-dark. And he *had* been behaving mega-suspiciously. None of which made me feel any better. Why must my life be so totally cringe-worthy?

The security chief jangled through his hefty bunch of keys to find the one for the handcuffs.

'We'll have you free in a sec, sir,' he said.

Oh, joy. A hired goon with a noseful of dust and a giant grudge against me, free and un-handcuffed.

'Rosie, love, are you all right?'

I looked up to see Nan hurrying towards me with Soph, Abs, Mrs Green and Louise.

'I'm fine,' I said, as Nan gave me a hug. 'What's going on?'

'We were about to ask you the same thing,' said Abs. The five of them gazed at me, the security guards and the goon on the ground.

'I'll explain later,' I mumbled, wondering if blushing clashed with green face-paint.

'It's all my fault!' said Louise, bursting into tears. 'I can't do this any more.'

'Do what?' said Soph.

I looked at the goon, who was sitting up, rubbing his wrists. His slick suit was covered in dust. He was staring straight at Louise, who was obviously terrified of him.

'I'm not doing it any more,' she repeated, sobbing. 'I don't care what you threaten me with, it's not worth it.'

She seemed to be talking to the goon. We waited for him to answer.

'I don't know what you're on about,' he shrugged.

'We saw you at her house,' said Abs. 'We know there's something going on.'

'We heard you telling her to pretend she didn't know you,' I said.

Louise sniffed. 'I'm not lying any more, so you may as well come clean.'

'This is all very confusing,' said Meanie Greenie. 'And this is hardly the most appropriate place to find out what's going on. Miss Parker, Miss Flynn, Miss McCoy, take Miss Collins and this gentleman to my office, please. And Mrs

Parker,' she added, although it was obvious she couldn't work out what Nan had to do with any of this. 'I need to make sure Miss Good is taken care of and make an announcement, but I'll join you shortly.'

* * *

'Well I never,' said Nan, ten minutes later as we all stood around in Mrs Green's office. 'I don't think I've ever been in a headmistress's office before.'

'I saw plenty when I was at school,' said the goon.

Big fat surprise, I thought.

Louise was still sobbing.

'Have a tissue, dear,' said Nan, pulling one out of her handbag.

Louise blew her nose.

None of us knew quite what to say. Mrs Green had sent along Mr Gregory, to make sure the goon didn't disappear before she got back. As we'd walked across the sports field to the school, we'd heard her ask the crowd to be patient, promising

Georgina would be on stage soon. Louise made a funny choking sound after the last bit. Mr Gregory had let us in to the office with Mrs Green's key and we'd stood around awkwardly ever since.

'So sorry to keep you waiting,' said Mrs Green, breezing in. She waved at a circle of chairs in the corner and said, 'Sit, sit.'

She dragged her chair over from the desk and we all sat down.

'Right,' said Mrs Green, calmly. 'Louise, I think we should hear from you first.'

Louise took a deep breath. 'I suppose it all started when I posted one of my songs on the Internet,' she said. 'I mean, I've been writing them for years, and singing, too, but I was always too shy to let anyone hear them.'

She paused and blew her nose again.

'I'd been visiting other people's pages on *MyPlace* and it seemed like an easy way of letting people hear your songs without actually having to perform them.'

'Nice and anonymous,' said Mrs Green.

Louise nodded. 'I decided to put up one song to start with and I used a fake name – SongBird.'

'*You're* SongBird?' I said, gaping. It seemed impossible that quiet, mousey Louise Collins could have such an amazing singing voice.

'I wrote "I Wish Things Were Different" last year,' Louise said, 'and it's me singing on the track. I hoped a few people might like it, but I had no idea it would get so much attention.'

'But if you're SongBird,' said Soph, 'who's Georgina Good?'

Louise choked back another sob and looked at the goon.

'After the song started to take off, I got an email from this really famous record producer who'd managed to track me down. He said I had real talent and he wanted to make me a star, so we arranged a meeting. But as soon as he saw me, he changed his mind.'

She was crying really hard now. Mrs Green leaned over and put a hand on her arm.

Louise sobbed, 'He said I had no star quality

and I wasn't pretty enough. I thought that would be that, but he said he still wanted to turn the song into a proper record – he just needed to find another SongBird. A prettier SongBird.'

'That's *horrible*,' said Soph, sounding as shocked as I felt.

It was all starting to fit together. 'It's you, isn't it?' I said to the goon. 'You're the producer.'

'Jack Chapel,' he said lazily. 'I've produced more hit records than you could download in a month of Sundays.'

'So he found another girl to sing your song?' said Mrs Green.

'He can't have,' I said. 'Louise sings on the track.'

'He said he didn't need to find another voice, just a different face,' said Louise. 'All she had to do was mime and look cool.'

'And that's where Georgina Good came in,' I said.

Louise scowled at Jack Chapel. 'She's his daughter.'

'That doesn't make any sense,' said Abs. 'If

you're such a big-shot producer, and your daughter wants to be famous, why not just find her a song and make a record? You don't need to steal someone else's song *and* use their voice.'

'Georgina can't sing,' said Louise.

'It's true,' shrugged Jack Chapel. 'I probably shouldn't say so, but she's utterly talentless. I spent a fortune sending her to the best stage-school in the country, but even after years of training, she's hopeless.'

'It's nice you're so proud of her,' I said. Mum's always telling me off for being sarcastic, but I couldn't help myself.

'Shocking, that's what I call it,' said Nan.

Mrs Green looked disgusted.

'What I still don't understand,' she said to Louise, 'is why you agreed to go along with it.'

'He said I had no choice,' said Louise, 'that no one would believe me. Everyone knows Jack Chapel, so I though he was right, and that people would think I was some crazed loser of a fan.'

'But what did *you* get out of it?' I asked.

Louise half-laughed. 'Money,' she said. 'And that so isn't why I write songs. I love doing it, I always have done. He said I'd get a share of the money and that I was good enough to make a living from songwriting when I leave school. It's all I've ever wanted to do,' she added, sadly.

'I can't believe you kept it all to yourself,' said Soph.

It was no wonder Louise had been so nervy and clumsy, or that she'd been off school for almost a week. Just looking at that slimy record producer was enough to make me feel a bit on the barfy side.

'I wanted to tell you what was going on when you found my notebook,' said Louise. 'You must've thought I was a total nutjob. But I was too scared.'

She gazed down at her lap, twisting Nan's tissue into a tiny ball. All of us, except Jack Chapel, were stunned.

'Louise,' I said, remembering something.

She looked up.

'When we saw *him*,' – *that idiot*, I wanted to say,

except Mrs Green was there – 'coming out of your house, he was carrying an envelope.'

Louise nodded. 'It was more songs. He made me record them and write out the lyrics. "I Wish Things Were Different" was doing so well, he wanted enough songs to record a whole SongBird album.'

Jack was still slumped in one of the armchairs. He barely even looked ashamed.

'It was a business deal,' he said. 'She got paid, didn't she?'

Nan tutted very loudly, but didn't say anything.

Suddenly, there was a knock at the door.

'Come in,' barked Meanie Greenie.

The door opened and two policemen walked in, followed by Mr Gregory. I hadn't even realised he'd left the room, I'd been so caught up in Louise's story.

'Sorry to interrupt, Mrs Green,' Ella's dad said, 'but I've taken the liberty of reporting this matter to my colleagues down at the station.'

'Jack Chapel?' said one of the policemen.

'Yes,' he said. For the first time he looked a bit uncomfortable.

'Mr Chapel,' said the policeman. 'Could you accompany me to the station to assist with our enquiries regarding SongBird?'

I realised Mr Gregory must've gone out to call the police as soon as Louise explained that Jack Chapel was blackmailing her. He caught my eye and winked.

'What enquiries?' said Jack. 'I haven't done anything wrong. It was a business deal.'

'Nevertheless, sir . . .'

'This is preposterous,' Jack stormed. 'Where's Georgina?'

'Miss Good has agreed to come down to the station. She's waiting in the car.'

'What about her?' said Jack, wildly, pointing at me. 'She attacked me!'

The policeman looked me up and down.

'With all due respect, sir, she's a quarter of your size and dressed as a cucumber. I hardly think she can have done much damage.'

'She's a frog,' Soph muttered, as they led Jack Chapel away. 'It's a *frog* costume.'

'Well,' said Mrs Green, standing up. 'What an afternoon!'

'I said there'd be a simple explanation,' Nan piped up.

'No, you didn't. You said they were planning to –' I mimed cutting my throat.

'Rubbish,' scoffed Nan. 'I always knew you weren't deranged,' she added, patting Louise on the shoulder.

'Right,' said Mrs Green. 'We'd better get going.'

'Going where?' said Louise, sounding alarmed. 'Do the police need to talk to me, too?'

'They might later, but not right now,' said Mrs Green. 'That wasn't what I meant.'

She pointed out of the window.

'There's a huge crowd out there waiting to see SongBird – and SongBird,' she smiled, 'is exactly who they're going to see.'

Chapter Ten

'Local Girl at Centre of Musical Mystery, by Lester Howard,' Abs read from the *Borehurst Chronicle*. Me and Soph were sprawled across my bed, listening.

'The school fête at Whitney High School became the centre of a major musical scandal on Saturday afternoon, when singing sensation Georgina Good was revealed to be a fake. Miss Good burst on to the music scene last month, claiming to be behind the mysterious hit by SongBird, "I Wish Things Were Different", but sources yesterday alleged she had only ever mimed to the song. Crowds who had waited for hours to see her perform were treated instead to the début performance from the real SongBird. Louise Collins, a pupil at Whitney High School, both wrote and sang the hit song, which hundreds of thousands of fans have downloaded from her website. Despite initial confusion, when Miss Collins found the courage to overcome her natural shyness and took to the stage to prove herself, her performance was a huge success, with the crowd demanding no fewer than three encores.

"Louise is a natural performer and has real talent," said head teacher, Mrs Miriam Green, and after the events of yesterday, your *Borehurst Chronicle* reporter would have to agree.

'Details of how the SongBird cover-up came about are sketchy at the moment, but it is believed Georgina Good left the school fête in a police car, along with a mystery man in sunglasses.'

'Lester Howard?' said Soph. 'Wasn't he that journalist who kept shoving in front of us to try and get closer to the stage?'

'Yeah,' said Abs. 'I think he was the one shouting, "SongBird, I'm your biggest fan," over and over again.'

'Way to act cool,' I said.

None of the journos at the fête had done a brilliant job of covering up their glee at being right in the middle of a major story. Up until then, most of them had hung around looking bored. When Meanie Greenie had announced we were about to see the first ever performance by the real Song-Bird, they'd perked right up. Me, Abs and Soph were standing in front of the stage and nearly got crushed as they pushed forward.

'Louise was très excellentissimo, though, wasn't she?' said Soph.

'It's still really freaky to think she's SongBird,' said Abs. 'Right there under our noses, and we didn't know.'

'I can't believe we got everything so totally wrong,' I frowned. 'We thought she was a mad stalker – but Georgina was making Louise's life miserable, not the other way round.'

'Her and Jack Chapel,' said Soph.

'I blame Nan,' I said, darkly. 'If it hadn't been for her stupid film about the deranged kidnapping fan, we'd never have suspected Louise of anything like that.'

'Then again, you probably wouldn't have done that flying tackle on Jack Chapel and got Louise to 'fess up, either,' said Abs.

'I thought we'd agreed never to mention the gun incident again,' I said.

Abs smirked. 'It was seriously hilarious.'

'For you, maybe. I, on the other hand, have learned my lesson about jumping to conclusions and will never do it again.'

They both stared at me and burst out laughing.

'What?' I said.

* * *

Life for me, Abs and Soph pretty much got back to normal after that. Time Lord gave me a three-hour lecture over my 'lack of professionalism' on stage during the play. Nan kept insisting she'd known all along there was something fishy about Georgina Good and Mum went on a few more dates with Unfunny Brian before she decided his nose hair was a deal-breaker.

None of us saw much of Louise – at least, not in person. After the fête, it wasn't just local newspapers that were interested in her. When Jack Chapel and Georgina Good were charged with blackmail a few days later, it was all over the tabloids and celeb magazines. Louise did hundreds of interviews, on TV and radio, too. At first, she was the same shy Louise we knew. Even under the TV make-up, you could totally see her blushing. But she gradually got more confident, and when they asked her about the fête (which all of them did, even though the entire world already knew the story), she'd talk about the nature reserve and why we'd invited SongBird to the fête in the first place.

'Louise has done a terrific job of raising awareness,' Mr Adams said, one morning in registration, 'and I'm delighted to announce that

Porter-McCabe are looking for a new site for their office complex.'

'You lie!' I said.

It just sort of popped out.

'Rosie, I guarantee you, it's the truth,' Mr Adams grinned.

'What's my dad always saying?' said Soph, as Mr Adams took the register.

'"Soph, get off the phone"?' I suggested.

'All's well that ends well,' said Soph. 'The nature reserve is saved, Louise's song has been number one for five weeks and that slimeball Jack Chapel is probably going to jail. Oh, and Amanda Hawkins has to be nice about Louise, even though it practically *kills* her, because Time Lord keeps saying he always knew she had star potential.'

'All good,' I said, reaching into my school bag, 'but don't forget this.' I pulled out a smart purple-and-silver card. 'We've been invited to Louise's album launch party at the weekend.'

'No way!' said Soph and then she looked a bit panicky. 'Did you say *this* weekend?'

I nodded. 'Why?'

'It's just, the weekend's only three days away. How the crusty old grandads am I meant to find the perfect outfit in three days?'

* * *

Clothes were not my biggest problem – Nan was. Louise had invited her to the party as well. Like I said, I don't make a habit of taking Nan out with me, especially when 'out' is a seriously cool party. It's not that I don't love her, but would you want to be seen in public with someone whose idea of partywear is a frilly blouse and a kilt?

'Heavens, this is posh,' said Nan, as we walked into the small, very cool club. The man at the door had checked her invite three times before he eventually let her in. 'I wonder if they've got any sausage rolls,' she said, trotting off towards the bar.

'Am I dead?' I asked Abs and Soph.

'Eh?' said Abs.

'I was just wondering, has the embarrassment actually done me in yet?'

Abs poked me in the arm. 'Nope, still here, facing the shame.'

'Look,' said Soph, 'we're just in time.' She pointed to a little stage in one corner. Louise had just sat down with a guitar and a man was adjusting her microphone.

The lights dimmed. Everyone clapped and cheered.

'Thanks,' said Louise. 'I'm going to play a couple of songs from the album.'

She sounded way more confident than before, and she looked amazing. She'd had her hair cut and, as Soph had predicted SongBird would, she was wearing jeans with a funky printed dress over the top. She launched straight into 'I Wish Things Were Different', which sounded even more amazing live than it did on the downloaded version.

'She *sooo* rocks!' Abs shouted in my ear as the song ended and we all erupted into applause again.

'The next song is called "Sometimes Wrong Is So Right",' said Louise. 'It's going to be my second single and I want to dedicate it to some really special friends who are here tonight – Rosie, Soph, Abs and Mrs Parker.'

Behind me, I heard Nan splutter into her glass of sherry.

'If it wasn't for them, I'd never have had the courage to tell anyone I was SongBird, and all of the amazing stuff that's happened to me over the last few weeks would have been impossible.'

'Wow,' said Soph.

'Such a sweet girl,' sniffed Nan.

It was every bit as brilliant as 'I Wish Things Were Different', and by the time she'd finished playing four more songs from her album, we were desperate to get our hands on it.

'I liked the one about the bags,' said Nan. 'It had a lovely tune. *I'm getting bags for Norman,*' she warbled.

I stared at her. Why do my relatives have to be so much more embarrassing than everyone else's, that's what I want to know?

'"I'm Getting Back to Normal,"' I said. 'The song was called "I'm Getting Back to Normal".'

'Yes, well,' Nan huffed, 'I thought it was smashing.'

'It's one of my favourites, too,' said Louise from behind us.

We all turned round. Louise had a massivo grin on her face.

'I'm really pleased you could make it,' she said.

'As if we'd miss this,' I said.

She looked like the old, shy Louise for a minute. Then suddenly she gave me a huge hug, before doing the same to Abs, Soph and Nan.

'I meant it,' she said. 'I couldn't have done it without you.'

'Yeah, cos every mega-successful pop star needs to be suspected of being a mad stalker,' I said.

She laughed. 'I *was* acting pretty weirdly.'

'So when are you coming back to school?' said Abs.

'Not for a while,' said Louise. 'I'm going on tour with Mirage Mullins. I'm just supporting her, but it should be really cool.'

'Oooh, Mirage is brilliant,' said Soph.

'So you wouldn't mind going to one of her concerts?' said Louise.

'Do the French like their cheese stinky?' I said.

Louise took some tickets out of her pocket and handed one to each of us.

'It's Mirage's concert, but I'm the support act,' she said. 'You have to come backstage afterwards. She really wants to see you again.'

Mirage is a singer me, Soph and Abs helped out a while back. It was crazissimo to think that we now had *two* famous songstresses for friends. We stood there looking like three stunned kippers.

'This is for you, Mrs Parker,' said Louise, giving Nan a theatre ticket. 'I didn't think Mirage would be your sort of thing.'

'*The Mousetrap*,' Nan read. 'Well, isn't that lovely? Thank you, dear.'

She kissed Louise on the cheek.

'It's a famous murder mystery,' she told us.

Quelle surprise.

'The play and the concert are on the same night,' said Louise, 'so I got my record company to arrange train tickets and a hotel for all of you, too.'

'All of us,' I said, suspiciously. 'Nan as well?'

Louise nodded.

Fan-blooming-tastic.

'We'll have a smashing time,' said Nan. 'A nice train journey and afternoon tea before your concert. I'll keep you out of trouble.'

Me, Abs and Soph looked at her.

As if that was *ever* going to happen.

Fact File

NAME: Amanda Hawkins

AGE: 14

STAR SIGN: Scorpio

HAIR: Brown

EYES: Brown

LOVES: Picking on other girls with her cronies Keira and Lara

HATES: The way Rosie, Soph and Abs always get to meet so many megastars

LAST SEEN: Sucking up to Time Lord

MOST LIKELY TO SAY: 'Me? Jealous? Never. You three are sooo tragic'

WORST CRINGE EVER: Starring as Juliet in the school production of Romeo and Juliet and sitting in some make-up before going on stage. She did the whole performance with big stain on her bottom and nobody told her until the end of the show. Quelle horreur!

What's your On-stage style?

Answer the questions to find out who you'd be in a Whitney High play

1. What's your secret talent?
a. What I lack in talent I make up for with enthusiasm!
b. *Secret* talent? Why would I keep quiet about it?!
c. I'm not sure I've found it yet!

2. What's your favourite outfit?
a. Jeans, a funky T-shirt and trainers
b. Anything involving sequins, feathers and heaps of bright colours
c. I'm not too bothered about fashion

3. What would you like to be famous for?
a. Anything – I just wanna be a celeb!
b. Starring in a musical in London's West End
c. Writing a number-one single

4. What do you like to do at the weekends?
a. Hitting the shops with my mates is a must!
b. My weekends are jam-packed with singing lessons, dance class and stage school
c. Chill out in my room and write songs

5. What would your perfect job be?

a. Writing for a celeb gossip magazine
b. Being a Hollywood starlet, of course
c. Working in an animal sanctuary

6. What kind of animal are you most like?

a. A puppy, because I'm fun to be around but can be noisy at times!
b. A cat, because I like it when people make a fuss of me
c. A bird, because I love to sing and have my head in the clouds

How did you score?

Mostly As:

Like Rosie and Abs, you're always involved in school plays because you think it's a real laugh. But how come you always end up in the most ridiculous costume?!

Mostly Bs:

Hey, you're a totally talented superstar! You love the limelight and are always centre-stage. It's a good job you're not as big-headed as Amanda!

Mostly Cs:

You might be shy like Louise, but you've got talent by the bucket-load. Let your inner SongBird soar and success will come your way!

Soph's Style Tips

You will need:

- A rectangular piece of card
- A ruler
- A glue stick
- Some scissors
- A photo or drawing

1. Fold the rectangle of card in half, then open it out again, like this:

2. Cut a window out of one half of the card, leaving a border around the edge.

The back of your card

Cut a hole a bit smaller than your picture

Find out how to make an awesome megastar photo frame!

3. Pop your photo or drawing over the cut-out window, put glue around the card surrounding it, then fold the card in half again so your picture is sandwiched inside.

The back of your picture

Put glue here

4. Now cut out some stars from brightly coloured paper and decorate your frame with them. You could add picture cut out from magazines for a celeb look, or some sequins and glitter for a touch of bling!

Megastar

Everyone has blushing blunders - here are some from your Megastar Mystery friends!

Rosie

My mum was getting all over-excited about a gig she and her band, the Banana Splits, were going to do. But on the day of the show, her friend in the band called up and said she was ill and couldn't make it. Mum was devastated and spent the rest of the day begging me to take her place. She bugged me so much that I eventually had to say yes, and I ended up spending Saturday night dolled up in an eighties outfit with terrible make-up on. Thank goodness the only person in the audience who knew me was Nan!

Abs

We had to do a presentation about the environment in Mr Footer's science class, and I drew a big poster to hold up while I was doing my talk. I folded it up and packed it in my school bag the night before. When it was time for my talk, I held it up in front of my class. Straight away, everyone burst into fits of laughter. The poster was covered in pink drawing of unicorns and princesses, and had 'Megan' scrawled all over it. My little sister is SO annoying and SO embarrassing!

Cringes

Soph

I made this awesome necklace to wear to the Whitney High disco. It was made from all sorts of special beads which matched my outfit perfectly. When we arrived at the disco, Rosie, Abs and me hit the dance floor straight away. I was really going for it when suddenly my necklace snapped and hundreds of beads bounced all over the place! My beads were lost and my face was bright red. As if things couldn't get any worse, I stepped on a bead and fell over right in front of my crush!

Louise

I've always been quite shy, so when Mr Adams said I had to read out one of my poems in assembly I was really nervous! By the time I walked on to the stage in front of the whole school, I was shaking. I walked to the middle of the stage, opened my mouth to start my poem and a huge hiccup came out! I had hiccupped five times before I had finished the first line, and I was as red as a beetroot. Luckily, Mrs Green saw the funny side and said I could read my poem another time!

SongBird's Online Profile

 SongBird Online now!

 Send message

 Add to friends

All about me:

Iím just a normal girl who happens to LOVE writing and singing songs!

All about me:

Hometown: Borehurst
Age: 14
Hair colour: light brown
Eyes: brown
School: Whitney High

Now playing:

'I Wish Things Were Different' – SongBird

Find out all about the girl behind the hit song

Blog:

Thanks to all my fans!
Hi guys – thanks for checking in on my personal profile! I promise to keep it updated with all my exciting news now that you know who I am!

read more

The real SongBird is revealed:

Meet Louise Collins, the face behind the music that everyone has been talking about.

read more

Comments:

 NosyParker: Loving your work!

 CutiePie: I never thought I'd be sitting next to the real SongBird in maths!

 FashionPolice: Louise, I can't believe you saved the nature reserve AND made Borehurst less boring!

MEGASTAR MIX-UP

Can you tell which characters' names are hidden in these word muddles?

PRIZE LARK

SPICEY MOOCH

RIB DONGS

FLABBY NINE

PERKIER SOAR

PAMPER ARK

Ten Reasons Why School Plays Rock!

How many more reasons do you need to get on the stage?!

1 Free rein in the costume cupboard. What do you wanna be: a glam fifties starlet, a magical fairy or an old man with funny teeth?!

2 It's a valid reason to skip lessons on rehearsal day – nuff said!

3 Helping out with the make-up could be your ultimate opportunity for revenge, especially if the star of the show has been getting on your nerves (every school play has its own Amanda Hawkins!).

4 You always knew that you had hidden talents, but no one believed you. Until now, that is . . .

5 . . . And there could be an agent in the audience waiting to discover YOU!

6 You're the star of the show AND the talk of the school.

7 Got a secret crush you've been dying to impress? He could be in the front row to see you looking your best!

8 You can pick up masses of brownie points with the parents for 'Getting more involved'. Maybe they'll stop hassling you now!

9 Your teacher won't go mad if your homework's a little bit late (not on the morning after the play, at least).

10 The after-show party is guaranteed to be BRILLIANT!

Pam's Problem Page

Never fear, Pam's here to sort you out!

Dear Pam,

I'm really shy and I hate it. Not only that, but I go red when I'm nervous which just makes everything worse. I've just found out that I have to sing a song in front of a massive crowd and I'm worried I'll go all shy and red again!

Louise

Pam says: I've got a funny feeling that you've got a lot of talent hidden behind that shy exterior, and my funny feelings are usually right. So, stop worrying about your performance and do something relaxing, like watching a few episodes of Murder, She Wrote with a nice cup of tea. Then, when you go on stage, just pretend to be Jessica Fletcher. She wouldn't get in a fluster, now, would she? You run along, sing your song and treat yourself to a custard cream afterwards. Everything will be marvellous, won't it?

Can't wait for the next
book in the series?
Here's a sneak preview of

Estelle

Chapter One

'Mmm, pizza is delicissimo,' I said, grabbing my fourth slice from the mound of food that completely covered the kitchen table.

'If you want any garlic bread, you'd better be quick,' Abs warned, as she piled some on to her plate.

'Oi! Leave me some, Abs!' said Soph. 'Got a vampire on your case or something?'

We were at Soph's house, it was Saturday night, and we were doing what we do best – watching a reality-TV show and commenting on all the contestants. Soph's parents were out at a party, so she'd invited us round. Normally, we took turns going to each other's houses at the weekend. I mean, we couldn't always be at my house, that was for sure. We'd all be driven slowly mad. Not only would my nan not let us watch what we wanted to (unless it happened to be a murder-mystery programme), but Mum would probably insist on inflicting her terrible taste in music on us. Seriously, the last time Abs and Soph set foot in the Parker household, they were scarred for life. Mum came into the room wearing disgustissimo leggings that caused Soph to have a serious fashion spasm, and Nan chuntered on and on about how great *Inspector Morse* is for so long that Abs nearly died of boredom. Sooo embarrassing!

Anyway, Soph's house is coolissimo to say the least. Her parents are pretty loaded, so they've got lots of très nice stuff. There's an amazing L-shaped leather sofa that's the size of a small island, and a seriously slick plasma TV. Soph's bedroom is way bigger than my lounge at home. Funny thing is though, Soph doesn't really notice stuff like that. She's definitely not snobby about it (unlike some people at school – like my arch enemy Amanda Hawkins), but what Soph *will* notice is what you're wearing. Example:

Soph: *Rosie, you've had that T-shirt for three years!*

Me: *So?*

Soph: *I can't believe you haven't done something with it. You know, like, customised it or something.*

Me: *Last time I tried that I ended up with an outfit that Mum loved – it was sooo not a good look.*

Abs: *Why don't you do something creative to it, Soph?*

Me: *Oh, no. No way, José. I am perfectly happy with it as it is. It's green, it has the words 'Rock Chick' on it – that's cool, isn't it?*

Soph: *Au contraire, mon frère. First, you are sooo NOT a rock chick. Second, it looks worn-in* *now, so you should fray up the edges to make it look a bit cooler. Third, you could maybe wear it with a skirt. Something other than jeans, anyway.*

You see? Soph thinks she knows everything about clothes. And everything about the person who wears them. Well, OK, she does know a lot about me. We've been mates, like, forever. But you'd think that by now she'd have got that even though I like clothes, I just don't care about fashion the way she does.

'Quick! *Stage-Struck*'s starting!' yelled Abs, who'd wandered back into the lounge during this thrilling discussion between me and Soph (she's only heard it about a million times before).

Me and Soph grabbed the last bits of garlic bread and raced into the lounge to take up our positions, me on the left, nearest the door. Dunno why, but I always have to be near the door. Maybe it's some kind of survival instinct I've got from living with my family – I often have to escape up to my room to keep my sanity. Like the time Mum and Nan got into this argument about who was more attractive – George Michael in his Wham! days or Detective Inspector Frost. They are totally nuts. Obviously the answer was neither. I started to worry that the inability to spot hotness was genetic, so I had to go upstairs and gaze at my Fusion posters to check that, yes, Maff, the lead singer, was still attractivissimo.

Anyway, Abs always sits in the middle, near the remote controls. She likes to be the one to use them, even if it's not her house. And Soph always sits in the corner of the 'L' bit of the sofa. I mean, it's not exactly comfy on the bum, but she likes being different. Still, we can all see the telly from our positions, so it works for us. This was the first episode of a show searching for the star for a new musical in London's West End, so it was important that we saw every detail. There were two big parts up for grabs – one male and one female – but there could only be one winner, so whichever part was left over would go to a professional.

'And now, let's meet the judges on our panel,'

the totally glitzed-up TV presenter, Daisy Finnegan, said. 'Anna Potter, the choreographer!'

'She's très strict,' Abs said.

'Yeah, but fair,' I pointed out.

'Next, we have the actor and singer Michael Donovan!'

'I'm loving his shirt/tie combo,' Soph said.

'What, yellow and purple?' I asked. *Gross.*

'Yeah, it's bold, it's bright –'

'It's barfissimo,' Abs finished.

'And, finally, we have the famous director of musicals, the man who will make this winner a star. Jeff Dalglish!' The presenter cooed at Jeff, who waved at the audience and the camera.

'Actually, he's not bad looking,' Soph said.

'Yeah,' I agreed. 'And he knows it.'

'And now let's see just how many people want to be a West End star!' the presenter cried. Then they cut to this film of people queuing up outside lots of different theatres and singing for the cameras. A doddery old man was doing a little tap dance routine and there was even one woman dressed as Mary Poppins. I mean, the lengths some people will go to just to get on telly!

'Hmmm. It's not going to be hard to whittle this lot down to only a few good 'uns,' I said.

'Oooh, harsh!' Abs said. 'Lucky you're not on the panel.'

'Au contraire, mon frère. I would be the voice of reason. I'd be no-nonsense, straight talking and full of kind advice. Like "Just stop singing already!"'

'Sssh. They're auditioning now,' Soph hissed, scanning the hopefuls' outfits. 'Seriously – have these people never heard of *Vogue*?'

For the next half hour we had a très fab time watching people embarrass themselves by attempting to sing, dance and – well, do *anything* in time to some music. Oh, the joys of reality TV! What the crusty old grandads did people watch before this?

'Tune in next week, when we'll have the first round of contestants singing live in the studio, and you can vote for your favourite,' the presenter said.

'Unless it's fixed from the start,' said Abs-the-cynic. 'You can tell the people they followed in this episode are going to get really far. Like Estelle.'

'Yeah, well, she *was* brilliant,' I said.

'And she's got a cool look going on,' said Soph. 'Maybe I should dye my hair raven black.'

'Yes,' I said. '*Or* you could make it like Jerome's – all long, lank and greasy.'

'Mmm, yes, *such* a good look,' Abs said. 'He was special.'

Soph shuddered. 'No way, José. Although he could sing quite well . . .'

'Yeah, so can Estelle. *And* she's written some songs of her own,' I pointed out.

'That's not always a good thing,' Abs said. 'Did you *hear* that Ivan bloke and his so-called "show tune"?'

An hour later, when Soph's parents came back after their party, we'd worked our way through everyone. Estelle was definitely our favourite.

'Hi, girls,' Soph's mum said, as she walked into the lounge. We whipped our feet off her posh coffee table. Mrs McCoy can be scary sometimes, but she's really très nice. 'Have a good evening?'

'Yes, thanks, Mrs M,' I said. 'You?'

'Yes, it was lovely. And I met someone rather interesting, Soph.'

'Oh, yeah?' Soph rolled her eyes and smirked at me and Abs.

'Your mother spent a very long time talking to him,' called Soph's dad from the kitchen.

Soph's mum looked a bit flustered. 'Oh, Richard, we were just *chatting*. He moved to Borehurst last week so I was telling him some stuff about the area.'

Soph sighed. 'I thought you said *interesting*, Mum.'

'Wait till you hear who it was,' her mother said. 'Jeff Dalglish.'

'What?!' the three of us shrieked.

'The judge on *Stage-Struck*?' Abs said.

'Yup. And he needs a babysitter next weekend. So I volunteered you, Soph.'

Soph leapt up and hugged her mum, then shouted, 'I'm going to his house! I'm going to his house!'

She flung herself at me and Abs and we all jumped up and down in a circle. Imagine! Soph babysitting for someone famous!!! Someone who'd been in the celeb mags so many times, I felt I knew his lounge really well already! After all, I don't just *flick* through *Star Secrets* magazine every week, y'know. No, siree. I remember every detail of every celeb shoot and interview they do. I carry a lot of interesting information around in my head, actually. For example, I know Jeff's wife, Melissa, is an actress. She was in one of those cop shows recently. And before that, she was a model. They met on a shoot for a magazine interview with Jeff. He had to have lots of women draped over him for the picture and Melissa was one of them. Since then, they've shown off their children (two) and happy home (gorgeous!) in various mags. And now Soph would be able to give me a first-hand account of what their new place was like!

'See, I *do* meet interesting people sometimes,' Soph's mum said, smiling. 'When Jeff asked me if I knew anyone who could do it at such short notice, I thought of you, Soph, of course. He hasn't got time to interview candidates, and he needs someone who's trustworthy.'

'This is sooo cool!' Soph said.

'I wish we could come too,' I said, wistfully. 'I'd love to see his new house.'

'Can we?' Abs asked. 'Do you think he'd mind? Three of us would be more responsible than one, after all.' That's what I love about Abs. She always comes up with convincing reasons to do stuff.

'Good thinking, Batgirl! He doesn't have to pay us,' I said. Soph nudged me hard with her elbow. 'Well, he could pay *Soph*, of course . . .'

'Si, si, it would be so cool if you could come too,' Soph said. 'Imagine hanging out at the Dalglishs' house!! Mum, d'you reckon he'd let us?'

'Well, I don't know. I can ask him, I suppose,' Mrs McCoy said slowly. 'I've got his number . . .'

'You've got his number?' I cried. 'Coolissimo!'

Soph's dad came into the lounge with two cups of coffee and shook his head at the sight of us all jumping up and down. 'I'd wait a bit before you call him,' he advised. 'The sound of all this shrieking won't encourage him to say yes.'

'No, call him now, Mum!' Soph said. 'While he's all pleased at having met such a nice person from Borehust. Go on, go on, go on.'

'Oh, all right then,' her mum said, going to the phone.

Me, Abs and Soph all grinned at each other and stood there, waiting to hear what he'd say. I grabbed Abs's hand for luck.

'Hello, Jeff? Yes, it's Mary McCoy. We just met at the Walkers' party . . . Yes, that's right . . . No, she can still babysit. But we were wondering if her friends Abigail and Rosie could help her? . . . Yes, they're experienced babysitters, too . . . I've known them for years. Very nice girls . . . We thought three would be better than one . . . OK, great! We'll let you know. Thanks! . . . OK, here she is.' Soph's mum gestured for Soph to come to the phone. Putting her hand over it, she whispered, 'He said it's all right as long as your parents are happy about it.'

Yes!!! Abs and I high-fived and did a victory

dance. We would definitely be able to convince our parents it was fine.

'Yes, sure,' Soph was saying. 'Thanks, Mr Dalglish . . . I can't wait to watch the show in your house! . . . Wow! Thanks! . . . Yes, see you next week.' She put the phone down and grinned at me and Abs. 'He says he'll see us next week at five and he'll get in loads of snacks for us!!'

Wow! We were going to the house of a famous director and a model-turned-actress next week!! Celeb heaven! And, if he gave us a bumper bag of sweets and treats, chocolate heaven too!! What could be better?